F
Carlson

Carlson, Melody.

Love gently falling.

DATE			

ALSO BY MELODY CARLSON

Once Upon a Winter's Heart

Love
Gently Falling

MELODY CARLSON

CENTER STREET

New York Boston Nashville

Center Street
Hachette Book Group
1290 Avenue of the Americas
New York, NY 10104

www.CenterStreet.com

Printed in the United States of America

RRD-C

First edition: January 2015

10 9 8 7 6 5 4 3 2 1

Center Street is a division of Hachette Book Group, Inc.
The Center Street name and logo are trademarks of Hachette Book Group, Inc.

The Hachette Speakers Bureau provides a wide range of authors for speaking events. To find out more, go to www.HachetteSpeakersBureau.com or call (866) 376-6591.

The publisher is not responsible for websites (or their content) that are not owned by the publisher.

Library of Congress Cataloging-in-Publication Data

Carlson, Melody.
Love gently falling / Melody Carlson. — First edition
pages cm
ISBN 978-1-4555-2810-3 (trade pbk.) — ISBN 978-1-4555-2809-7 (ebook) 1. Love stories. 2. Christian fiction. I. Title.
PS3553.A73257L68 2015
813'.54—dc23
2014007339

Love
Gently
Falling

Chapter 1

Rita woke with the lovely dream still fresh in her mind. Gracefully gliding across a shimmering ice rink illuminated by a rainbow of light, she'd felt unencumbered and free and weightless...as if she were flying. Getting out of bed, she pulled on a pair of fuzzy socks and, extending her arms, slid across the hardwood floor as if she were really on ice, as if she could spin and leap and execute moves she hadn't attempted in years. She skidded to a fast stop by the window, pausing to open the blinds, allowing the Southern California sunshine to flood into her pale blue bedroom. Not exactly a winter wonderland.

As she gazed down to the pool area, where tall, graceful palms barely moved in the morning breeze, she vaguely wondered if a public ice rink was even located in Beverly Hills. And even if a rink was nearby, would she be bold enough to pay it a visit? Twenty-nine seemed a bit old to reinvent oneself as a figure skater.

Not that she'd ever been much of a skater. Rita chuckled as she threw the comforter back onto her bed. Truth be told, she'd probably spent as much time on her hind end as she'd spent on her skates, but it had been fun. And not a bad way to grow up... back in Chicago. Continuing to slide her feet, she faux-skated out into the great room of the condo. Swaying side to side, she moved smoothly across the hardwood, attempting a couple of awkward moves as she worked her way toward the kitchen. She knew this was silly and wouldn't want her roommates to witness her antics, but Margot would be at work by now, and Aubrey was probably still asleep.

"What on earth are you doing?" Aubrey asked with what sounded like way too much amusement.

Spying her roommate in the shadows of the hallway with a foaming mouth and toothbrush in hand, Rita just shrugged. "Ice skating."

"Good to know." Aubrey laughed. "I heard the clunking and got worried that we were having an earthquake."

"And here I thought I was being so graceful," Rita said sarcastically. She was well aware that, with her nearly six-foot frame, grace was not her strong suit. And with petite and delicate roommates who lovingly called her Moose sometimes, it was a fact she was mindful of.

As Rita went into the kitchen to start a pot of coffee, she tried to remember how long she'd been sharing accommodations with Margot and Aubrey. It was shortly after she'd landed her job as a stylist at Roberto's... which was almost seven years ago. She'd felt on top of the world back then—being in her early twenties and working for one of the chicest salons, living in an upscale neighborhood with a couple of pretty cool roommates. How much better could it get for the daughter of a Chicago car salesman and a hair-dresser?

Margot, the oldest of the roommates, owned this condo unit and hadn't raised the rent once. A corporate attorney, she was as dependable as they came. Aubrey was a year younger than Rita and could be a little unpredictable at times, but she was generous and fun. And since she worked for a fabulous restaurant in the neighborhood, she could always be counted on to bring home something divine at the end of her shift. Rita's contribution was free beauty advice and sample products. All in all, it was a pretty good setup for all three single girls.

And yet, as Rita poured water into the coffeemaker, she felt restless. Maybe it was just the remnants of her ice-skating dream, slowly melting away in the warmth of the California sun. Or maybe it was something else. She sighed as she turned on the small flat-screen in the kitchen, tuning it to the local news, where, according to Vince the weather guy, it was going to be "another unseasonably warm day." Not a record breaker, but in the high eighties. And to think this was late January!

"So what's up with *ice skating*?" Aubrey asked as she came into the kitchen and opened the fridge.

Rita sheepishly explained her dream. "It felt so real. And it was so awesome to be gliding along like that. Made me want to go ice skating again." She paused to sneak a cup of coffee from the machine as it brewed.

"Were you a pretty good skater?"

Rita laughed. "Not really. But I enjoyed it. That dream was probably just a subconscious reminder that I've been missing winter."

"You probably should've gone home for Christmas." Aubrey filled a glass with orange juice. "I hear it's been seriously cold in the Midwest."

"Yeah. My mom said they had a really pretty white Christmas." Rita sighed to think of snowflakes tumbling down, ice sculptures, a rink filled with skaters wearing woolly hats and mittens and scarves... "I don't suppose there's an ice rink in Beverly Hills... is there?"

"I don't know about that, but Culver City used to have a good rink. We kids went there sometimes when I was growing up. My sister still lives in Culver. Want me to ask if it's still there?"

"That's okay. I don't really have time for ice skating this week anyway." Rita glanced at the kitchen clock. "In fact, I should be getting dressed. I have a nine o'clock appointment this morning." She held her coffee cup toward Aubrey. "What're you doing up this early?"

Aubrey pointed at her teeth. "I lost a crown last weekend. I have a dentist appointment at ten."

As Rita reached for a banana, the landline phone jangled. Assuming it was a telemarketer, since few of their acquaintances used that particular number, Rita ignored the ringing as she peeled her banana. But after the message beep, it was her father's urgent voice that made her dash to the phone, grabbing up the receiver. "*Dad?*" she asked frantically. "What's going on?"

"Oh, Rita," Richard said with a smidgen of relief. "I'm so glad I reached you. I tried your other phone number and no answer. And now this one, and I was about to give up and call your work number." He paused to catch his breath. "Anyway it's about your mother. I don't where, how, to begin, but—"

"What's wrong?" she interrupted. She knew how her dad

could go on and on sometimes. "Please, Dad, just cut to the chase and tell me what's happened!"

"Your mother has suffered a stroke."

"A stroke?" Rita tried to absorb this. "When did this happen?"

"Last night. The doctor said it happened while she was asleep. She must've slept right through it. I didn't know anything was wrong until early this morning."

"Is Mom *okay*?"

"No, not really. I mean, she's alive, Rita. But she's *not* okay. She's not herself at all."

"Where is she?"

"Jackson Park Hospital. That's where I am right now. She's in ICU, and they're doing all they can for her—lots of tests and God only knows what else. But she's in a bad way, Rita."

"A bad way?" Rita reached for a barstool, easing herself onto it. "What do you mean, Dad? Is she going to make it?"

"I don't know—" Her dad's voice broke, and she could tell he was crying. Rita could only remember him crying once before—when his mother, Grandma Jansen, had passed away. "I really don't know what's going on with her, honey. The doctor said the worst is probably over, but your poor mother can't talk or walk or eat or anything." He made a choking sob. "It feels like she's already gone."

"*Oh, no!*" Tears filled her eyes. "I've got to come see her, Dad."

"I know, honey. I thought you'd want to come. Do you need me to send money for airfare or—"

"No, Dad," she said firmly. "You don't need to do that." She knew that, thanks to the economy, her parents had been more financially strapped than ever. For that reason she'd been extra frugal with her own earnings. "I have money... my savings," she reassured him. "I'm fine."

"All right, then." He let out a weary sigh. "Call and let us know when you'll get here. I still don't have a cell phone. Can't stand those things. So you can either call your mom's phone, which I'm on right now, although I barely know how to use it. Or, better yet, call your brother."

"How's Ricky doing?" She knew that her younger brother had been struggling a lot recently, still adjusting to the after-effects of some serious football injuries he'd sustained while playing college ball last year. Poor guy.

"Oh, Rita, Rick's taking it pretty hard. Your mom's been such a help to him this past year... and now this."

"I'll be there as soon as I can," she promised. "And I'll do whatever I can to help."

"Thanks, honey. I hate interrupting your life like this, but we really do need you."

"Don't worry, Dad. I'm on my way."

As Rita hung up, she turned to see Aubrey still in the kitchen. "Oh, Rita," Aubrey said with worried eyes. "I didn't mean to eavesdrop, but is it your mom?"

Rita nodded as she grabbed a paper napkin to wipe her tears. "It's a—a stroke. It sounds like she's not even conscious. My dad was really upset. He thinks she might not make it."

Aubrey hurried over, wrapping her arms around Rita. "I'm so sorry. What can I do to help? Want me to go online and book a flight for you?"

"Can you?" Rita asked between sobs. "My credit card is in my wallet, over there on the table."

"Absolutely. Do you fly into O'Hare?"

Rita nodded then blew her nose. "I need to go pack."

"And I'll let Margot know," Aubrey called out. "Want me to contact your work, too?"

"No, that's okay, I'll call the salon," Rita hurried to her room to get dressed, make plans, and let her tears flow freely.

Thanks to Aubrey's unexpectedly efficient help, Rita was on her way to LAX by noon.

"That was really nice of you to give me a ride," she told Aubrey's current boyfriend, Maxwell. "I told Aubrey I could get the shuttle, but she wouldn't hear of it."

"Hey, it's no problem," he assured her. "I was heading out to Westchester for a job anyway." Maxwell was a plumber, something Margot had mercilessly teased Aubrey about. But as he carefully navigated his way down Santa Monica Boulevard, Rita began to see him in a different light. Maxwell seemed like a genuinely nice guy. She suspected there was more to him than his faded jeans, sleeveless T-shirt, multiple tattoos, and well-worn work boots. And she knew he was trying to get her to relax and think positively.

"I know it seems dark to you right now," he said as he drove down the San Diego Freeway. "But medical technology is really amazing these days. I had an aunt who had a stroke a few years ago and she completely recovered. It just takes time and work."

"I'm sure you're right." She nervously fingered her electronically generated boarding pass.

"Your mom will probably need a physical therapist and a speech therapist. Does she have good insurance?"

"I think she does." They continued discussing all the ins and outs of stroke recovery, and by the time Maxwell took the LAX terminal exit, Rita felt unexpectedly encouraged. She also felt that Aubrey had surprisingly good taste in boyfriends—something Rita couldn't necessarily claim for herself. The last guy she'd dated had turned out to be a complete jerk.

She thanked Maxwell once again as he pulled up to the Jet Blue entrance. "Not just for the ride," she said as he helped her with her bags. "But the encouragement, too. It means a lot to me. You've been great. Really great."

"I'll keep your mom and you and your family in my prayers," he told her as he closed the back of his van.

She tried not to look surprised by this. Why wouldn't a nice guy like Maxwell be inclined to pray? "And I'll keep Aubrey posted about how it goes," she promised as she wheeled her bag onto the sidewalk and waved. "Thanks again!"

Once inside the bustling terminal, she began to feel overwhelmed again. But with no time to waste, she hurried through the various stages of getting to her gate. With every step Rita felt more and more like she was in a hazy dream. Not the sweet, happy dream she'd experienced this morning. This was more of a chilly, unsettling dream, where everything was fuzzy and blurry. By the time she reached her gate, her flight was already boarding, but she took a minute to call her brother's phone, leaving him a message regarding her flight schedule. "It'll probably be close to nine by the time I get my bags, and I'll just take the train from O'Hare to the hospital," she explained. "I know it'll be late at night by the time I get to Jackson Park. But I don't mind. I just want to be with Mom. And I do not want you or Dad coming to pick me up. *Understand?*"

Rita had no idea how Aubrey had managed to secure her a seat on a nonstop flight at such short notice, but she appreciated it. And the seat wasn't half bad either. Still, it was hard to sit patiently for four hours. And one could only pray for so long without feeling redundant and pathetic, not to mention not very faithful. Naturally, she'd been too worried and hurried to pick up anything to read. Plus the battery in her Kindle was dead. Left to the in-flight magazines and her own thoughts, she tried to remember the last time she'd been home. When had she last seen her mother...and her family? She felt dismayed to realize it had been a full three years. No wonder she missed snow and winter so much!

She tried not to send herself on a guilt trip for not having been home for so long—or for missing this past Christmas. Besides, she reminded herself, she'd been encouraging her family to come out and visit her this winter, promising them some warm California sunshine. In fact, the last time she'd talked to her mom, on New Year's Day, she'd sounded quite positive about making the trip, declaring that she wanted to see Disneyland. "Before I'm so old that you have to push me around in a wheelchair and spoon the applesauce into my mouth." They had both laughed over that then. It didn't seem funny now.

Rita didn't often admit it, but her mom had probably been her greatest mentor. Other than a couple of rough adolescent years, they'd remained really good friends. Rita had grown up watching Donna efficiently running her own business. Not only did she own and manage her own hair salon—Hair and Now—she was also an excellent and respected hairdresser, with a faithful following of clients. As a child, Rita had loved helping out at Hair and Now on no-school days. And when she'd announced her decision to go become a hairdresser, during her senior year, her mom had supported her. Even when Rita had to break the news that she'd chosen a beauty school in Southern California, her mom had still supported her. And she'd paid Rita's tuition. "Your grandmother gave me my start with Hair and Now," she'd told Rita. "This is the least I can do for you."

Rita had fond memories of Hair and Now. It was located on the lower level of Millersburg Mall, a mall that had once been host to one of the best ice rinks in the area—the same rink where Rita had learned to skate. But due to bad management and expensive repair costs, the rink had been shut down when Rita was in high school. The ice had been replaced with bistro-style tables and chairs and potted trees circling a big fountain. Many considered this an improvement, but Rita had always felt it was a mistake.

Hair and Now remained in the same place, where it had been nearly as long as the mall itself, and although Donna sometimes joked about retirement and had been preparing to celebrate her big six-oh next month, Rita had never gotten the impression that she was serious about hanging up her scissors. In fact, Rita had been convinced that her mother, with her sparkly blue eyes, youthful complexion, and shiny platinum-blond hair, was young for her age. When Rita was a teenager, she and her mother had sometimes been mistaken for sisters. "Oh, that's just because our coloring is so similar," her pragmatic mother would say in a dismissive sort of way. But Rita knew that her mom had loved the gaffe. And why not?

As announcements were made about preparing for landing, Rita felt a surge of conflicting emotions rush through her. She peered nervously out the window, looking through the dark night, down to where the blue-hued lights illuminated the landing strips of O'Hare. As much as she hated to admit it, she felt fearful that her mother might not have made it. What if she'd taken a turn for the worse and hadn't survived the day? But at the same time, Rita felt hopeful, remembering Maxwell's encouraging words about stroke recovery. Surely her mother, who'd always been a strong woman and a fighter, would still be holding on. Perhaps she'd be sitting up in bed by now, talking and joking with Ricky and her dad. Rita also felt a giddy sort of excitement to think of this—she was about to see her family again. But even that was laced with dark thread of concern. What if she was too late? What if her dad and Ricky were brokenhearted with grief right now?

Chapter 2

As she hurried down to baggage claim, Rita considered calling Ricky or her father, just to say she'd arrived
and to check on her mom's status. But she didn't want to
make them feel they needed to leave the hospital to come
fetch her. She was a big girl. She knew how to ride the
train...how to take a cab. She could make her own way to
the hospital.

Still, by the time she dragged her well-stuffed wheeled
bag from the carousel, she felt overwhelmed. The prospects of
hauling her baggage to the train stop, waiting by herself for
the next train, getting her luggage onto the train, riding all
the way into the city at this hour of night, then getting off
and finding a cab to take her to the hospital...well, it wasn't
for the weak of heart. But she could do it. She would do it.
She would do it for her mom.

"*Rita?*" a masculine voice called out.

As she proceeded to the exit, Rita glanced all around, expecting to see her brother's big ruddy face or maybe her dad's. But no one looked familiar. Perhaps she'd heard wrong...or maybe it was just wishful thinking.

"*Rita Jansen?*" the voice called out again.

She peered through the faces in the crowd by the door and spotting a handwritten sign waving above the heads, she was shocked to see her name clearly printed on it. "What is going on?" she mumbled to herself as she pushed through the travelers to investigate.

"*Rita!*" a tall man eagerly declared as he placed his hand on her shoulder. He wore a brown leather jacket, a red Bulls cap, and a big friendly smile. "I would recognize you anywhere."

"*What?*" Rita peered curiously into the man's face. He had warm brown eyes and was a few inches taller than her. "Do I know you?"

"You used to," he said cheerfully. "We went to school together. John Hollister. Remember?"

"*Johnny Hollister?*" She slowly nodded with recognition. "It *is* you."

"Yep." He reached for her wheeled bag.

"But what are you doing here?"

"Your brother asked me to pick you up."

"Ricky knows *you?*" She felt confused. "It can't be from school. I mean, Ricky is eight years younger than us and he—"

"I met Ricky through work." John lifted the carry-on bag from her shoulder so that she now only had her handbag to carry. "And your mom is one of my clients. I was real sorry to hear about her stroke today."

"Yes...me too." She frowned. "This is so unexpected."

"Anyway, Ricky told me to let you know that your mom

is already starting to improve a little," he said as he pressed their way through the crowd. Loaded down with her luggage, he led the way toward the exit.

"Thanks, but you didn't have to do this, Johnny. I planned to take the train and—"

"I wouldn't let my worst enemy ride the train into the city at night." He stepped aside, waiting for her to go through the door ahead of him. "And I should warn you that the hospital's located in an area that's not exactly safe." He held up her carry-on bag. "And with all this baggage, you'd be like a sitting duck for a thief."

As Rita got further outside, she was caught off guard by the cold blast of air that hit her. Pushing the collar of her lightweight jacket higher, she hurried with Johnny across the street. "It's freezing out here," she muttered as they went into the parking area.

"Yep. It's been hovering around twenty degrees these past few days." He chuckled. "Not like LA, eh?"

"Not in the least." She dug in her handbag for a silky scarf, wrapping it around her neck a couple times for warmth. "I forgot how cold it can get." As she picked up the pace to keep up with his long strides, she wondered about this morning's longing for winter. *Am I nuts?*

"Here we are." Johnny stopped behind a red and white utility van, and, after opening the back, he quickly set her bags inside. "Hopefully it's still warm inside. Go ahead and get in. It's open."

As she hurried around to the passenger's door, she read the words on the side of the van. Apparently Johnny worked for some kind of a janitorial service located in Chicago. "*Jolly Janitors?*" she said as Johnny slid into the driver's seat and started the engine.

He chuckled as he fastened his seat belt. "That's right. The way I know your mom and brother is from cleaning Hair and Now at Millersburg Mall. I've been doing her salon for a couple of years now."

"Oh..." She nodded, trying not to feel too judgmental. After all, what was wrong with a man working as a janitor? Good, honest work—and somebody had to do it. As Johnny maneuvered the large van out of the parking lot, she was hit with the irony of something. She had been driven to LAX in a plumber's van and now she was being driven away from O'Hare in a janitor's van. Okay, it wasn't very stylish or impressive, and Margot would probably have a good time teasing her for it. But really, a ride was a ride...and, as her mom would say, beggars should not be choosers. Besides it was far better than riding the train on a cold winter's night.

She glanced over at Johnny. And, really, despite being a janitor, he'd be rather attractive with his curly sandy brown hair, strong chin, and nicely shaped nose. Okay, he *was* attractive. And why was she being such a snob about it? She wasn't really like that. Was she? But for some reason it was hard to imagine being involved with a janitor. Why was she even thinking about something like this in the first place? For all she knew, Johnny was married with three children. Besides, she reminded herself as she turned her focus back onto the street ahead of them, she should be thinking about her mother right now.

"So...you say my mom is doing better?" she asked cautiously.

"Yes. That's what Ricky told me this evening when I dropped some flowers by for her. She's been moved out of ICU and into a regular room. And it sounds like she made good progress in her physical therapy today."

"She's *already* having therapy?" Rita wasn't sure which was more surprising—that her mom had been in therapy on her first day in the hospital, or that a Jolly Janitor had taken her mother flowers.

"Ricky said that they don't waste any time with stroke victims. The sooner she starts regaining her skills, the better the prognosis."

"So is she walking and talking?" Rita asked hopefully.

"No. Nothing like that yet. But it's just the first day."

"Oh...yeah..." Rita rubbed her hands together for warmth.

"Ricky suggested that I take you home," Johnny said tentatively as he turned the heat up. "He thought you'd be worn out from your flight and—"

"I really need to go to the hospital," she firmly told him. "I want to see my mom as soon as possible. That's why I came today. I know it's a ways farther than my parents' house, but if you don't mind, I really want to see her tonight."

"Sure...no problem."

"I'm guessing that Dad and Ricky are the ones who are worn out by now. They must be stressed and tired from being at the hospital all day. My dad hates hospitals. Maybe I can relieve them so they can go home and get some rest. I don't mind spending the night in the hospital with my mom. I really don't think she should be alone."

"I understand completely. I'm sure I'd feel the same if it was my mom."

She glanced over at him again. She'd always liked Johnny in school. He'd been one of the good guys—dependable and solid and kind. But he'd also been a little bit boring, too. Or so she'd thought back in high school. She felt a bit surprised he worked for a cleaning business, but only because she'd always thought he was more academic.

"I don't think we've talked since we graduated. Did you go to college?" she asked, partly out of curiosity and partly to make conversation.

"Sure did. Graduated from Northwestern in business. Six years ago."

"Oh... that's great. Good school."

"According to Donna—your mom, I mean—you graduated from a pretty impressive beauty school in Los Angeles."

Rita shrugged. "Most people don't think that beauty school's very impressive, but it was a good school. And I did land a pretty great job in a Beverly Hills salon."

"Really? Beverly Hills?" He nodded. "Ever work on anyone famous?"

"As a matter of fact, I have several well-known clients."

"Anyone I'd have heard of?"

"Well, I don't make a practice of name-dropping," she said a bit primly. "Clientele privacy, you know."

"Sure. That makes sense."

She appreciated that he didn't push her like some people did, and for some reason it made her trust him more. "But if you promise not to tell..."

He chuckled. "Scout's honor. And I really was a scout, too."

"Since you don't live down there, I guess it can't hurt." And so she told him a couple of the bigger names.

Johnny let out a low whistle. "Wow... now that's impressive."

She smiled with satisfaction. "I like to think so. Some of my clients swear that I'm the best colorist in Beverly Hills. But I like cutting and styling, too."

"I guess the apple doesn't fall far from the tree." He grinned at her as he waited for the light to change to green. "And I mean that as a compliment, Rita. I have nothing but respect for your mom."

"Thank you." She nodded. "I do take that as a compliment." For a while they just drove in silence, with Rita watching for familiar sights.

"You didn't make it to our ten-year reunion last year."

"I know. I really wanted to go, but I was busy with work."

"I heard it was because you were busy with a new boyfriend," he said teasingly.

"Who told you that?"

"Your mom."

"Seriously? My mom talks to you about my personal life?"

"I was on the reunion committee, and we hadn't heard back from you, so I thought maybe we used the wrong email. So I asked your mom and she set me straight. But she also told me why you weren't coming."

"Well, my mom didn't get it exactly right. It wasn't because I had a new boyfriend. It was because the guy I was dating was a cameraman—you know for films—and he kept acting like he could get me on as a hairstylist for a movie he was working on. It was all supposed to go down about the same time as the reunion. And I've always dreamed of working as a stylist on a film. So I gave up going home for the reunion in the hopes I'd get on with the film."

"Did you?"

"Nope." Rita let out a frustrated sigh. "As it turned out the guy didn't have as much influence as he'd insinuated."

"Oh...is he still your boyfriend?"

"No, but not because of that." She heard the sharpness in

her response and regretted it. It wasn't Johnny's fault that Ben had been a jerk.

"Sorry," Johnny said quickly. "I'm being too nosy again. It's my worst habit, and I'm trying to break it. I'll get to talking with clients, and the next thing I know I've stepped over the line by inquiring about their personal lives. My bad."

"It's okay." Rita smiled. "To be honest, I've been known to do the exact same thing."

"But you expect that in a hairdresser, don't you? I mean, I always hear about how hairdressers always get to hear the juiciest secrets. Kind of like you're in a special club."

"I suppose that's true."

"But with janitors...well, they're supposed to just scrub the floors and take out the trash and keep their big mouths shut." He laughed. "At least that's what I hear."

"You mentioned the reunion..." Rita began cautiously. "Do you recall if Marley Baines—I should say Prescott—was there or not?"

"Sure. Marley was there. But I'd think you'd have known that. You and Marley used to be best friends. Don't you keep in touch?"

"Not as much as you'd think." She frowned to think of how close she and Marley once were...a long time ago.

"Really? When was the last time you spoke with Marley?"

"Oh, it's been a while..." Rita bit her lip.

"Oh, well, friends sometimes grow apart..."

"Do you see her much?"

"As a matter of fact, I do. She's a client of mine as well."

"You clean Marley's house?"

"Actually, it's her business. She's got a thrift shop in Millersburg Mall. It's called Secondhand Rose. And she does a nice little business with young fashion-minded and frugal women."

"Come to think of it, my mom mentioned that to me. Kind of slipped my memory. So how is Marley doing?"

"Ah, so now you want me to divulge a client's private information?" he said.

"Oh, no, of course not. Sorry. I just—"

"Kidding. Well, I guess Marley is doing...uh...okay. Business is good anyway."

"Meaning her personal life isn't?"

"I didn't say that, did I?"

"No, of course not." Rita wondered how well Johnny really knew Marley. "It's just that, well, the reason Marley and I parted ways was because I was opposed to her marriage."

"Really?" he glanced at her. "You mean because they were so young? Just one year out of high school?"

"No. Well, I suppose that was part of it. But I actually spoke out against Rex. And subsequently I was uninvited from the wedding."

"Seriously? You dissed her fiancé?"

"I know...I know. I thought I was so smart back then." Rita shook her head to remember how she'd stuck her size eleven foot in her mouth. "It's embarrassing to admit now. Especially since Marley and Rex have been happily married for ten years."

"Happily?"

She turned to peer at him. "Aren't they?"

He shrugged, but she could tell by his expression that he knew something. "Sorry. Me and my big mouth again. Just pretend I didn't say that. Okay?"

"Okay..."

"Now if you're worried that I'll tell someone about your

impressive Beverly Hills clientele list, you can just threaten to blackmail me over that little slip of the tongue."

"Well, you've certainly gotten me curious now. If Marley and I were speaking to each other, I'd just pay her a visit and ask what's up. As it is, she'd probably slam the door in my face."

"Oh, I doubt that. Marley's a very savvy businesswoman. I don't think she'd slam the door on anyone who walked into Secondhand Rose. At least not while customers were around."

Rita considered this. That actually wasn't such a bad idea. "You say her shop's at Millersburg Mall? Where exactly is it located?"

"On the top level. A few doors down from Martindale's Department Store. In fact, Marley's shop is right next door to someone else you might remember."

"Who's that?"

"Zinnia."

"Zinnia Williams?"

"That's right." He nodded. "She just opened it last year."

Rita cringed to remember the uppity young woman who had worked as a receptionist for Rita's mom. Although only a couple years older than Rita, Zinnia had always treated Rita like a child. Even after Rita had landed her rather impressive job in Beverly Hills and come back home to celebrate, Zinnia had acted unimpressed and superior. "So... Zinnia has a shop... right next to Marley's?" she said quietly.

"Sure. And Zinnia and Marley are pretty good friends too."

"Seriously?"

He laughed. "I know what you're thinking. I heard Zinnia used to have a knack for rubbing people the wrong way. Fortunately, some people change."

"You're saying Zinnia has changed?"

"When was the last time you saw her?"

Rita thought about this. "I guess it was quite a few years ago. Back when she worked for my mom. What kind of shop does Zinnia have?"

"A hair salon."

"My mom told me about a new hair salon at the mall. But she didn't mention it was Zinnia's. Mom was mostly concerned because she thought it was in breach of her lease contract—you know, that there could only be one hair salon in the mall. Apparently it wasn't."

"I think the salons have to be located a certain distance apart." He pointed ahead. "And speaking of distance, here we are. Jackson Park Hospital at your service. How about if I deliver you to the front door?"

"Thanks! That would be lovely." Rita braced herself for the cold again.

"And I'd be happy to drop your bags at your house, if you'd like. It's not far out of my way and—"

"No, that's okay," she said as she opened the door, letting a frosty blast of air inside. "I'll ask Ricky to stash them in his car." She hurried around to the back of the Jolly Janitor van, waiting as Johnny extracted her baggage. But instead of handing them over to her, he ran them up to the door and inside the foyer.

"Tell Donna that she's in my prayers," Johnny said as he slid the strap of her carry-on onto her shoulder. "You all are."

"Thank you," she told him. "For everything."

"I know it's not terribly elegant riding around in the Jolly Janitor van." He grinned. "But it was the best I could do on short notice."

She smiled. "It was just fine, Johnny. And it was warm. And the company couldn't have been better."

He made a mock bow. "Thank you very much."

With a parting wave, she wheeled her bag through the lobby. She knew her focus should be on locating her mother, but for some reason her mind seemed stuck on Johnny.

Chapter 3

As Rita sat in the semidark hospital room, she replayed the moment when her mom had opened her eyes a couple of hours ago. Donna's expression had been so happy and bright that for a moment Rita forgot that she'd suffered a serious stroke. Of course, the lopsided smile was reminder enough. Combined with the fact that her mother was unable to form actual words. Donna had moved her lips and made some sounds that may have made sense to her, but sounded like baby talk to Rita. Even so, Rita had clasped Donna's hand, assuring her that things were going to get better.

"I hear that you've already made good progress," Rita had told her. "I'm so proud of you." Then she'd leaned over and kissed her mother's cheek. "I love you, Mom. We're going to get you well." After that she'd simply chattered at her mom, talking about the warm weather in California and her uneventful flight and how the Jolly Janitor had picked her up at O'Hare. The flickering in Donna's clear blue eyes made Rita believe she understood. And that gave her hope.

But watching her mother now was rather unsettling. Seeing her lying there so pale and helpless and motionless...with something still inside of her...something unknown and menacing that had brought on this stroke...well, it was quite disturbing. Rita knew from talking to the young intern on duty that nothing certain had been revealed in any of her tests yet.

"We feel relatively sure it was a hemorrhagic stroke," he'd explained. "Especially since she has no history of high blood pressure, high cholesterol, or heart disease. She's not obese, and she's never been a smoker."

"So that's good?" Rita had asked hopefully.

"It's good in predicting it wasn't an ischemic stroke. And if we're right and it was a hemorrhagic stroke, the likelihood of recurrence is reduced."

"So it could recur?"

"That's always a possibility. Something we can't ignore, even if it is hemorrhagic stroke, because it could've been caused by a blood clot. So far the scans haven't revealed this. And we've ruled out aneurysm. But she's scheduled for another MRI tomorrow morning. That may reveal something." He shared a bit more information (perhaps too much information, because it started to get a bit murky in her mind), but the friendly intern seemed to enjoy showing off his expertise.

As she thanked him for his help, she was curious about his age. Her guess was that he was younger than her, and, although she was wearing flats, he was shorter, too.

"If you have any questions or concerns, please, feel free to call. The nurses know how to reach me." He pointed to his nametag. "Some people are always looking for *Mister* Right. Well, you just remember, I'm *Doctor* Wright." He laughed like this was funnier than it was, and she suspected it was a line he'd used before.

Just the same, she thanked him, assuring him she wouldn't forget his name.

"And I'll hunt down some of the most current information about hemorrhagic stroke for you," he promised. "I can tell you're one of those people who like to be properly informed."

"Yes," she'd told him. "I believe that knowledge is like power." But as she sat here with her mother, she felt powerless. Besides praying and waiting, there seemed to be little that could be done. But at least she'd convinced her dad and brother, after an hour or more of a bittersweet reunion, to go home and get some rest. It had been nearly midnight by the time they finally left, and her dad had looked so worn out that she'd felt concerned for his health. "Make sure he goes to bed," she'd whispered to Ricky. "Even if he has to take one of Mom's over-the-counter sleeping pills."

Rita checked her watch. It was almost three a.m. Even on California time, she would've been asleep for an hour or two by now. She put the recliner chair back as far as it would go, willing herself to get a little shut-eye, but her mind was still racing with what-ifs. What if her mom didn't recover? What if she died? What if her dad's health went downhill as a result of all this stress? What if Ricky, who'd already been battling depression, got worse? What if? What if? What if? Finally, she knew her only recourse was to pray...and hope for sleep.

When Rita awoke, it took her a moment to figure out where she was. But seeing a nurse with a hypodermic needle in hand quickly brought her to her senses. The nurse was injecting something into her mother's IV tube. Probably meds to keep more blood clots from forming. Dr. Wright had mentioned something about that. Next the nurse checked her temperature and blood pressure and a couple of other things.

"How's she doing?" Rita whispered as she extracted herself from the chair.

"Her vitals are normal." The nurse checked something on the IV unit, then gathered her things to leave.

Rita peered down at her mother, wishing she'd open her eyes and smile again, but instead she just slept peacefully. And perhaps that was good. Maybe she needed the rest. Assured that her mother was okay, Rita decided to pay the restroom down the hall a visit. And while there, she would brush her teeth.

The hospital corridor was eerily quiet, and most of the patients' rooms were darkened, as if everyone was still sleeping. Passing by the nurses' station, she was relieved to see that at least the nurses were awake and chatting happily among themselves. The whole office area was decorated with glossy red and pink hearts and crepe paper and rosy-cheeked cupids—reminding Rita that Valentine's Day was only three weeks away. And that reminded her of how the week before Valentine's Day was always a busy time at Roberto's. It seemed that half of Los Angeles was ready for a makeover by mid February. Rita knew this was partly due to the Oscars—which usually happened about a week or two after Valentine's Day. Anyway, it was a fun time to be a hairdresser in Beverly Hills.

Taking her time in the restroom, Rita stood in front of the mirror, assessing the damaging effects of a four-hour flight and a mostly sleepless night. As someone in the beauty business, she was well aware of the toll these inconveniences could take on one's appearance. And the unforgiving fluorescent light was not helping. Fortunately, she'd had the good sense to keep her carry-on bag in the hospital with her. Ricky had taken the larger one. But everything she needed for beauty first-aid would be in here. Some might think her shallow for caring about appearances, but she knew that her mother would appreciate it as much as she would.

First she brushed the fuzzy sweaters off of her teeth. Next she ran a brush through her tangled shoulder-length hair and even rubbed some macadamia oil conditioner into the dry ends. She put eyedrops into her bloodshot eyes, then decided to take full advantage of the unoccupied restroom by giving her face a good invigorating scrub over the sink. She patted her skin dry, then slathered on a liberal coat of her favorite moisturizer, giving it plenty of time to soak in before she carefully applied her makeup. She completed her makeover with a squirt of a light-toned fragrance and a fresh shirt.

Feeling much better and satisfied that she'd made some much-needed improvements, she zipped her carry-on shut and returned to where her mom was still sleeping. She poked around for a few minutes, positioning the pretty flower arrangements so that they could all be seen from her mother's bed. There were red roses from her dad, a potted African violet from Ricky, pink roses from the Jolly Janitors—*That company must really care about their clients*, she thought—and a bouquet of spring colored tulips from Hair and Now. But seeing that her mother was not stirring, Rita decided to run downstairs and seek out a good cup of coffee.

Rita had just ordered a latté when Dr. Wright came over to greet her. "You look bright and fresh this morning," he said as he refilled his coffee cup. "How's your mother doing?"

"She was sleeping when I left her. She slept pretty soundly all night."

"That's good. Sleeping is nature's way of helping her brain to heal."

"Will she be sleeping a lot during the daytime too?"

"She needs a balance of rest and rehab therapy."

"And I know she's got that MRI scheduled for this morning." Rita reached for her latté.

"Yes. And I did print out some information about strokes. If you walk with me, I'll pick it up for you."

"Sure," she agreed. "I'd appreciate that."

"My shift is actually over," he explained as they walked. "Now I get to go home and get some sleep."

"I think I slept a total of three hours last night," she confessed.

"You should probably go home and get some rest too," he told her.

"Except that *home* is in California." She sighed to think of the comfortable memory foam bed she'd left behind—and the old squeaky twin bed she'd be sleeping in tonight.

"A California girl." He gave her an appreciative nod. "Whereabouts?"

"Beverly Hills."

He looked impressed. "Nice. I'll bet the weather's a little warmer there."

"That's for sure." She told him about the unseasonable weather.

"So where will you stay while you're in Chicago?" he asked with what seemed a little more than professional interest.

"At my parents'."

"Oh, right." He paused by a door marked PRIVATE. "I'll grab that printout now."

As she waited for him, she wondered if Dr. Wright was flirting with her. It wasn't like this was something new. For some reason a lot of guys seemed to be attracted to tall blond women. Unfortunately, they often turned out to be the wrong kinds of guys...something that Rita was still grappling with.

"Here you go." He handed her some papers and, looking directly into her eyes, he smiled. "Hopefully, I'll be seeing more of you. I'm back on duty tonight at six. Think you'll be here then? Maybe we could sit down with coffee and discuss your mom's prognosis."

"I don't know if I'll still be here." She glanced away, unsure of how to react. Was he hitting on her? "I mean, I plan to stay as long as I can today. But I need to get some sleep."

"Well, I'm on the night shift all week. I'm sure our paths will cross again." He reached into his pocket and removed a business card. "If you need to reach me, this has my number."

"Thanks." She nodded. "I didn't realize doctors had business cards."

He laughed. "Sure, why not? How about you?"

"What?"

"No business card?" He looked disappointed.

"Oh, yeah." She reached into her handbag, digging for the pocket where she kept a handful of cards from her salon. "I have this."

"Roberto's Spa and Beauty Salon?"

"I'm a hairdresser," she told him.

His fair brows shot up. "A hairdresser?"

She stood straighter, looking down on him slightly. "That's right. Just like my mother. We do people's hair for a living, and we happen to like it."

"I'm sorry. I'm just surprised. I didn't mean to sound disapproving."

She made a forced smile. "Yes...I'm used to that reaction. But our clients are very appreciative."

"Yes, I'm sure they are." His pale gray eyes twinkled. "I suspect it's similar to how patients feel about their doctors."

She nodded briskly. "In some ways it probably is." Now she glanced at her watch. "I better go. My mom might be awake by now and I don't want her to be alone." She made a little finger wave. "See you around, Doc."

He chuckled. "I hope so, Rita. Give your mom my best," he called as she walked away.

She wasn't sure why she felt aggravated as she rode the elevator up. Really, she should feel flattered—a doctor was flirting with her. Wouldn't her mother be pleased? And yet she felt something about Dr. Wright was insincere. And his reaction to finding out she was a hairdresser? Well, that had seemed fairly revealing too. Despite his denial, he had seemed to clearly disapprove. Or maybe she was just tired...and being overly sensitive.

Finding that her mother was awake and sitting up, Rita put thoughts about Dr. Wright aside and focused her attention on her mom.

"How are you doing?" Rita asked slowly and clearly, like Ricky had explained she should.

Donna mumbled a response, reaching for Rita with her left hand—the one unaffected by the stroke. She squeezed Rita's fingers and smiled happily, mumbling something unintelligible.

"I'm so happy to see you, too," Rita said in response, hoping she'd read her mother correctly. She reminded her about the MRI scheduled for nine o'clock. "But it's still early." She

pointed to the clock on the wall. "Almost two hours before they'll come get you." She held up the printout that Dr.
Wright had just given to her, explaining what it was. Then,
hoping to amuse her mother, she confided her suspicions that
the intern was flirting with her. "I could be wrong, but it
seemed pretty straightforward."

Donna's eyes twinkled as if she really understood this.

"Don't tell me you had this all planned out?" Rita said in a
lighthearted tone. "Get yourself into the hospital so that your
daughter can hook a doctor?"

Donna actually laughed about this. Then she muttered
something that Rita could not make out at all. Donna tried
again, but it was even worse. Naturally, this frustrated her
mother even more than it frustrated Rita.

"It's okay," Rita assured her as she flipped over to the page
she'd skimmed earlier, the one about speech problems, or
aphasia. Some suggestions she already knew—like speaking
slowly and clearly and not talking down to the person having
difficulty. But it also suggested asking questions that only re-
quired yes or no for answers, allowing the patient to nod or
shake her head. Rita asked several questions like that and her
mother's relief at being able to communicate—even if it was
very basic—was a good reward.

"It also says here that you might be able to draw some
pictures to communicate something," Rita explained to her
mom. "You'd have to use your left hand for now. But it might
be worth trying. I'll pick up a notebook in the gift shop."

Donna nodded with eager-looking eyes.

"Looks like your breakfast is coming," Rita told her as a
cart was wheeled in.

"Would you like to help her with this?" the nurse's aide
asked Rita as she carried a tray to the bedside table.

"Sure. Any suggestions?"

"She's had difficulty swallowing, so just encourage her to go slow. Everything here is liquid so it should be fairly easy for her to get it down. But it takes time."

And it did take time. Especially since Donna insisted on trying to feed herself with her left hand, which was clumsy. But Rita did her best to remain patient, only helping when it seemed really necessary. And after about an hour, her mother was finished. But she pointed at Rita. Pantomiming with her left hand, like she was eating again.

"You think I should go eat breakfast, too?" Rita asked.

Donna nodded eagerly.

"I had a latte already. But now that you mention it, I guess I'm hungry, too."

Donna waved her hand toward the door.

"But I hate to leave you."

She waved her hand again, giving Rita that strong, motherly I-mean-it look.

Rita laughed. "You might be half paralyzed, but you still know how to get your way, don't you?"

Donna smiled. And just then Richard and Ricky came into her room.

"Good timing," Rita told them as they all hugged. "Mom is kicking me out." She quickly explained and even gave them the sheet about working through aphasia before she left.

As she went down the elevator again, she felt a heavy sadness coming over her. Her mother was really trying, but it seemed clear she had a long, hard road ahead. According to what Rita had read this morning, recovering from a stroke of this magnitude took time. It might be six months or more before her mom was even partway back to normal ... and even that wasn't for sure. Rita had asked her manager, Vivienne, for two weeks off, but she knew that time was going to zip by. Perhaps it would be wise to let them know she might need a little more time. Fortunately Aubrey had gotten her an open-ended ticket, because Rita knew she wouldn't want to leave Chicago before she felt certain her mother was making real progress.

Chapter 4

Later that day, not long after Donna returned from her MRI, Grandma Bernice came to visit the hospital. "I would've come sooner," she told Rita. "But your dad said to wait until they were done with all Donna's tests and whatnot." She peeked into the room. "How is she doing?"

"She's resting right now. I think the MRI wore her out a little," Rita explained. "Dad and Ricky just went out to get some lunch. You can go in and sit with her if you want."

Grandma Bernice nodded. "Yes, I'll do that. But tell me the truth, Rita, *how* is she?"

Rita shrugged. "Well, she has no use of her right arm, and she can't talk. She understands what you're saying, but she can't really respond—not intelligibly anyway. She gets frustrated. And she has some trouble walking, too, but the doctor thinks that will improve in time. I guess we'll know more after today's test results are read."

"And her spirits?"

"She's in surprisingly good spirits," Rita said. "But she's always been such a positive person. I guess it makes sense she'd be a trooper about this too."

"And is she out of the woods? From what I've read there's always a chance it can happen again."

"The doctor said that each day after the stroke increases the odds that she won't have another one. But this is only day two."

Grandma Bernice hugged Rita again. "Oh, it's so good to see you, darling. I wish the circumstances were different, but you are a sight for sore eyes."

"Thanks." Rita patted her grandmother's snow white curls. "And, as always, you look very pretty."

"Well, no matter our age, we have to look our best."

"Speaking of that, Mom had me do her makeup after she came back from her MRI."

"Did she really?"

"Yes. She couldn't say it in so many words, but she did a pantomime and I knew exactly what she meant. So be sure to tell her she looks pretty, okay?"

"Well, of course I will. And since I'm here and all ready to sit with my girl, I insist that you should go join the fellows for lunch."

Rita didn't argue with her grandmother. She knew better. She also knew that her mom would be delighted to see her own mother. Hopefully she'd wake up soon.

By Donna's fourth day in the hospital, everyone was beginning to feel a bit more hopeful. All the scans had come out clean, and the prognosis for a recurrence of stroke seemed slim. Besides that, it appeared that the damage caused by the stroke wasn't as extensive as the doctors had first assumed.

She still had almost no use of her right arm and her speech was greatly impaired, but already, thanks to intensive rehab therapy, she was making progress—both speech and physical. Besides being able to walk unassisted and use the toilet without help, she was able to make sounds that resembled *yes* and *no* as well as several other simple words. Baby steps, perhaps, but encouraging.

"At this rate, we should be able to discharge Donna by Monday," Dr. Jane Morrison told Rita and her family on Thursday afternoon. "With the recommendation that Donna continues her rehab from home, since I understand that's Donna's preference." Dr. Jane smiled at Donna. "Right?"

"Yeah." Donna nodded with enthusiasm.

"And Ricky and I will be there to help her while Dad's at work," Rita assured the doctor. "We've got it all figured out."

"I'll drive her to rehab therapy," Ricky said. "And I'll make sure she does her exercises." He grinned at Donna. "Right, Mom?"

"Yeah." She nodded again. "Righ..."

After Dr. Jane left, the four of them continued to visit a while longer, and then, as Donna's dinner arrived, Ricky and Rita excused themselves to go home, allowing their parents the rest of the evening to visit in private. Rita had been touched by how tender her dad had been as he engaged with her mother. She'd always known their devotion to each other was genuine—the kind of love story that endures through the ages—but seeing her dad helping her mom like this now, tenderly wiping a bit of soup from her chin or pushing a strand of hair from her eyes...well, sometimes it was hard to hold back the tears.

"I'm glad Dad went back to work today," Rita told Ricky as he drove them home. "But I can tell he's really worn

out from this week. I hope it won't be too much for
him—working and visiting Mom at night. I mean, he's not
exactly a spring chicken."

"Don't let Dad hear you say that," Ricky teased. "He says
that today's sixties is like yesterday's fifties."

"I hope so...but look at Mom. She's not even sixty yet."

"But that was a fluke. Nothing to do with her age."

"Still, I can't imagine what we'd do if both our parents got
sick."

"Well, at least Dad has weekends off now," Ricky pointed
out. "One of the few perks of his job change."

Rita was well aware that the automotive industry had
taken its toll on her dad's job situation. Instead of selling new
cars, he now worked in the service department. Not actually repairing vehicles, but managing the desk on weekdays.
Although he still got the same benefits package, which was
important considering Donna's recent hospital stay, his salary
had been reduced significantly. It was just one more reason
that her mom had been unwilling to retire.

"Mom wants me to go to Hair and Now tomorrow," Rita
told him. "To see how things are going."

"She *said* that?"

"Well, not in so many words. It was partly from what she
drew on the drawing pad and partly from me asking her yes
and no questions. But it's obvious that she's worried about the
business. I told her that I'm happy to fill in for her. I can take
her appointments as long as I'm here."

"I've talked to Charlene every day since Mom got sick,"
Ricky said. "Giving her updates, you know. But as far as I can
tell, business is pretty slow."

"That may be, but I promised Mom I'd go in tomorrow. So
that's what I plan to do. And you don't need to take me over

there. I'll just use Mom's car. So you'll be on your own with
Mom at the hospital all day. Do you mind?" Rita had noticed
how much Ricky had been limping today. She knew that his
leg and back were hurting him.

"No. Of course, not. I already planned to go."

"And don't overdo it," she warned. "Use that recliner in
Mom's room to put your feet up. Take a nap if you need to.
Or just play your silly video games."

"Wow, you're giving permission?" Ricky chuckled. "And
are you going to tell me what I should tell Dr. Wright when
he comes looking for you?"

Rita rolled her eyes, remembering how Dr. Wright had
stopped them on their way out this evening. Clearly he had
more than just chitchat on his mind. "Tell him whatever you
like."

"Hmm . . . what if I tell him that you're really into him and
that you're just waiting by your phone for him to call?"

"You better not!" She reached over and playfully punched
his arm.

"Kidding."

"Thanks a lot, bro."

"Seriously, that dude seems like he's really into you, Rita."

"Appearances can be deceiving."

"Hey, some girls would be gaga over the prospects of a *doctor* boyfriend."

"Yeah, my roommate Margot would be impressed," Rita
admitted. "But something about Dr. Wright feels all wrong
to me."

"Yeah, he seems a little *too smooth* to me." Ricky turned into
their driveway. "Kinda *slimy*."

"Okay, that's a bit harsh." Rita wrapped the woolen scarf
that she'd borrowed from her mom's closet around her neck

as she climbed out of the car. Hurrying up to the house, she wondered if she'd ever acclimate to the extreme temperature change.

"Looks like the church ladies have been here again." Ricky picked up the cardboard box sitting on a chair by the front door. "Wonder what's for dinner?"

"That's really sweet of them to do that." Rita unlocked the door. "I wonder how long they'll keep it up."

"We've already got enough leftovers to last a couple more nights." Ricky carried the box into the kitchen. "Maybe we should just freeze this."

"If it's not already frozen from sitting out in the cold." Rita turned up the thermostat before she started to peel off the top layer of winter clothes. Then, as usual, she went around attending to the household chores—playing mom. If her mother was really coming home on Monday, it might be time to give the whole house a thorough cleaning. It seemed neglected. As they ate dinner in the kitchen, she explained her plan to deep clean. Although Ricky's enthusiasm was lagging a bit, he agreed to do his part. And by the time they called it a night, they'd actually made a pretty good dent on the place.

The next morning, Rita was eager to get over to Hair and Now. She hadn't been to the salon in years and was looking forward to rolling up her sleeves and helping out with some of her mom's clients. She knew the salon didn't open until nine, and that Charlene had been doing that, but since she had her mother's keys, she decided to get there early and open it herself. Her plan was to surprise the girls by picking up a box of Krispy Kremes on her way. This kind of treat would not be appreciated where she worked in Beverly Hills—everyone there was always on some sort of weird diet—but here in the Midwest, well, she didn't think anyone would mind.

Besides that, she told herself as she carried the cardboard box through the freezing cold to the back door of Hair and Now, all of this cold winter weather had to burn a few extra calories. She unlocked the door and let herself into the back room, pausing to absorb the familiar smell. The faint aroma of ammonia mixed with her mother's favorite vanilla deodorizer combined with some pine-scented cleaning solution transported her straight back to childhood. "Welcome home," she said as she turned on the lights.

She set the box on the counter between the washer and dryer and, surveying the tidy surroundings with everything neatly in place, she removed her coat, scarf, and gloves, hanging them in the closet by the back door. Nothing in here had changed. She turned the thermostat up a bit then went into the main part of the salon, flipping on the lights and taking a quick inventory of the cutting stations. Everything in here was the same, too.

The chairs were the same dusty rose color that her mother had chosen to redecorate with when Rita was a little girl, although the vinyl had some stains and tears—signs of years of use. The station tables were the same oak that had been fashionable in the nineties—more worn and out of style perhaps, but still serviceable. The pale gray linoleum on the floor was the same, but definitely showing signs of wear. In fact, it was actually peeling in places. The walls were the same, gray wainscot below with a dusty pink faux marble paint above. Fashionable three decades ago, but so ho-hum now. All in all, Hair and Now looked rather old and sad and shoddy. Especially compared to where Rita worked.

Just the same, Rita knew that her mom loved this place.

She always had. And she probably wouldn't want to change a thing. At least that's what she used to say when Rita was a teenager and full of ideas for salon upgrades. Among other things, Rita had wanted Donna to put in a mani-pedi station as well as a spray-on tanning booth, but she wanted to keep the salon strictly hair. Rita had also wanted her to change the color scheme. But her mom had insisted that the pink shades were feminine and soothing. Just the same, Rita wondered how her clients felt about it now. What if the rundown appearance cast a negative light on their level of service?

"*Hello?*" a woman's voice yelled sharply. "Who's in there? Identify yourself before I call the police!"

"Hey, Charlene, it's just me," Rita called back. "It's Rita!"

"Oh, Rita." Charlene came in grasping her buxom chest with both hands as if she were having a heart attack. "My word! I thought we were being burglarized."

"I'm sorry. Didn't you see Mom's car out there?"

"I saw it, but I know Donna's still in the hospital. So I wondered if someone had stolen it and was breaking in. You know they've had some trouble around here. In fact, just last week I was telling Donna we should get a security system installed."

"Seriously?" Rita grimaced over the dismal surroundings. "What would a thief possibly want to take from here?"

Charlene frowned. "Well, you never know." Now she came over and giving Rita a big bear hug, she pulled her tightly into her well-padded body. "It's so good to see you, girl. How's your mother? I saw her on Wednesday, and Ricky gave me updates yesterday. Anything new?"

"Not really. But she's making daily progress, and it looks like she can go home on Monday."

"That soon?" Charlene unbuttoned her winter coat.

"She'll have to continue rehab therapy from home. But Ricky is determined to help with that."

"Probably be good for them both. That boy needs to stick with his physical therapy, too."

Rita picked at some loose piping on a chair. "This place looks a little rundown, Charlene. I don't remember it being this bad last time I was here."

Charlene shrugged. "Yeah...but that was a while back. And money is tight and upgrades are spendy."

"Do clients ever complain?"

"Why should they complain?" Charlene looked indignant as she smoothed her short auburn hair into place. "They get quality hairdressing at an affordable price. If that means we can't decorate like they do in *Beverly Hills*, our patrons shouldn't complain—*should they?*" She gave Rita the exact same look she used when Rita was a teenager questioning something in the salon.

"No, no...of course, not."

Charlene's tone softened as she led the way to the back room. "Sorry, honey. Didn't mean to bite your head off. But it's been a bone of contention lately. A couple of our best hairdressers quit last fall...complaining that we're not keeping up with the times. *Irksome.*"

Rita wanted to say she could understand why a good stylist wouldn't want to work here, but she knew that would offend Charlene—as well as be disrespectful to her mom. And she wondered...really, what was the point? As hard as it was to think about, how likely was it that her mom would return to work anytime soon? Or ever, for that matter?

"So what are you doing here?" Charlene asked as she hung up her coat.

"I brought Krispy Kremes," Rita announced brightly.

Charlene laughed. "You came out here this early just to bring doughnuts?"

"Actually, Mom asked me to come. She wants me to help out."

"She's talking now?"

"Not exactly." Rita explained how they communicated.

"How does she want you to help out?" Charlene opened the dryer and removed a load of towels, starting to fold them. "What are you going to do, exactly?"

Rita reached for a towel, folding it as she considered her answer. "To be honest, I'm not really sure. But Mom seemed pretty determined and urgent. She wouldn't take no for an answer."

"I've been handling her appointments." Charlene reached for another towel. "It's not like we're real busy, Rita."

"Why not?" Rita set her folded towel on the small stack.

"Well, winter is always a slow time of year."

"Oh...?"

"And have you heard about *Zinnia's?*" Charlene made a sour face.

"Yeah..."

"Well, I'm sure that's eaten a good portion of our business."

"That makes some sense." Rita considered the salon's shabby condition again, wondering why Charlene couldn't see how uninviting it was. It certainly wasn't the kind of place Rita would feel comfortable getting her hair done in—well, unless she knew the people running it. But even then. A woman liked to feel special and pampered and important when she got her hair done. Hair and Now just couldn't provide that anymore.

"I've got a lady from the nursing home coming here for a

perm at nine thirty," Charlene told her. "I should probably start getting things set up." She chuckled. "Well, as soon as I sink my teeth into one of those yummy doughnuts."

"I'll make the coffee."

"Good girl."

"And then...I want to go over everything, Charlene. I want to study the appointment books and the inventory and the computer programs and everything. I want to see if I can come up with a business plan."

"A business plan? Well, wouldn't that be something." Charlene took a bite of a doughnut and smiled at Rita. "Maybe you're just what this place needs, honey."

Rita wondered about that. Was she really what Hair and Now needed, or would she simply end up irritating everyone with her ideas and suggestions and criticisms—the same way she used to do?

Chapter 5

Rita parked herself at the reception counter with a cup of coffee as she studied the appointment book and some outdated computer programs, making notes of ideas that might improve business. She remembered the days when Hair and Now had employed a part-time receptionist—Zinnia— during the busiest hours of the day. Apparently that practice had gone by the wayside, too. One of Zinnia's responsibilities had been to keep track of the inventory of beauty products on the nearby shelves. But judging by the faded labels of bottles and tubes, everything on this shelf was probably at least ten years old. It should all be thrown out. Perhaps it could be considered a tax loss.

Around midmorning, the two part-time hairdressers showed up. Rita hadn't met them before and cheerfully introduced herself, but they both regarded her with suspicion and a general lack of enthusiasm. Clearly, they were not overjoyed to be employed here.

"There are Krispy Kreme doughnuts in back," she told them in a friendly tone.

"Just what this figure needs." Jillian patted her thick midsection. "More sugar."

"Not that it will stop you," Yolanda teased. "It never has before."

"Just because you can eat anything and stay thin..." Jillian glared at Yolanda.

Before long, the two of them returned with their doughnuts, loitering around the reception area as if they were curious about the new interloper. "So you're the hairdresser to the stars," Yolanda said to Rita. "Donna talks about you all the time."

"Most of my clients aren't celebrities," Rita clarified. "But, yes, I do work in Beverly Hills."

"How's that compare to here?" Jillian asked as she chewed a bite of doughnut.

"Naturally, it's different." Rita glanced around the lackluster salon and sighed. "I have to admit that I was a little surprised at how rundown Hair and Now has gotten."

Well, that comment opened the floodgates, and suddenly Jillian and Yolanda started unloading long laundry lists of everything that was wrong with this salon. Fortunately, their appointments—a pair of elderly women—showed up, and they had to get to work. But Rita made notes of some of their more legitimate complaints. And when they weren't busy with customers, she invited them to list things they'd like to see changed and give them to her. She doubted they'd come up with anything she hadn't already observed, but she knew it would make them feel validated. Plus it would strengthen her case—which she planned to present to her mother.

As she finished dumping the dated beauty products, after

listing their retail values for tax purposes, she realized it was past one and she was hungry. She told the other women she was going out for lunch and even offered to pick them up something, but with no takers, she got her coat and hurried out the front door. To her surprise, instead of the court-yard she remembered, she found some sort of construction was in process. Men and noisy tools and dust seemed to be everywhere. She knew that the lower level of the mall was considered the less valuable real estate, but with all this mess going on, it felt like the slums. She rode the escalator up and was immediately struck by how different the atmosphere was on the upper levels. She could still hear a little construction noise, but the piped music helped to camouflage it a little. And the shops up here looked light and bright and shiny and new. Many of them had inviting Valentine's Day displays in their windows. And the general feeling was of prosperity and success. So different than down below.

Rita went into Noah's Ark, which was located directly above Hair and Now. She hadn't been in here in years, but remembered how it had been a fun hangout when she was a teen. To her surprise, the original owner, Noah Goldstein, was standing behind the counter. "You're still here," she said happily.

"You bet." He grinned at her. "Good to see you, Rita. I heard about your mom. How's she doing?"

Rita gave him the update, then, as a couple more cus-tomers got into line, she placed an order for soup and bread and took a seat over by the back wall. She smiled to see the old Noah's ark mural still there, complete with the colorful rainbow above it. Her friends used to say, "meet you under the rainbow," when they were headed here. And she used to jokingly tell her mom that Hair and Now was located beneath the rainbow, saying that it was like the pot of gold. It had seemed true then, when business was good. Not so much now.

As Rita ate her beef and barley soup, she wondered what was to become of her parents. She knew that Ricky's injury had depleted what little savings they had, and that her dad's decreased salary wasn't sufficient to support them without the additional income from the salon. She also knew that since the business wasn't thriving and her mom leased her space, there was nothing to be gained from selling Hair and Now. If only there was a way to fix it up. Rita considered her own savings, which she would gladly donate to help her parents, but she knew it wasn't enough to make a real difference. What Hair and Now needed most was a miracle. Maybe she should buy a lottery ticket.

As she waved goodbye to Noah, she decided it was time to pay her old best friend a visit. Johnny had said Marley's thrift shop was near Martindale's. That should be easy to find. As she walked past the various shops and stores, she noticed that a few spaces were vacant. Not as many as there had been the last time she'd walked through here—about five years ago. Hopefully the economy was picking up.

"Secondhand Rose," she read the curly lettered sign out loud as she paused by the glass door. Marley's middle name was Rose, and sometimes, when they were little girls and playing dress-up, Marley would go by Rose. Rita peered in the storefront window, where a stylish selection of romantic outfits was artistically displayed. She marveled at the enticing layers of lacy tops and floral scarves and velvet vests and flowing skirts and a variety of interesting accessories—all in complementary shades of pink, magenta, red, and lavender. Perfect for Valentine's Day.

A bell jingled as she pushed the door open and stepped inside. At first glance, she could see the shop was charming. And if a person didn't know, they would probably never even guess it was a thrift store. It even smelled nice...an exotic mixture of spice and floral tones, but not too heavy.

"Welcome," a cheery voice called out from the back of the store.

Rita caught her breath as Marley emerged from behind the counter, smiling and looking retro-chic in a short burgundy dress with black textured stockings and tall boots. *"Rita!"* Marley's dark brown eyes grew large in disbelief.

"Marley..." Rita felt a lump in her throat, wondering what she should do. Pretend to be shopping? Apologize? Make a run for it?

But before she could decide, Marley rushed toward her, threw her arms around Rita, and hugged her tightly. "Oh, Rita! I've missed you so much."

"Me, too," Rita said with a sob. "I'm so sorry, Marley. So sorry I said what I said back then. I was so stupid and immature and I was probably just jealous and—"

"Oh, hush!" Marley stopped her. "As it turned out, you were right."

Rita frowned. "I'm sorry."

"Yeah...so am I." Marley stepped back to look at Rita. "My elegant Beverly Hills friend has arrived."

Rita touched her hair. "I sure don't feel very elegant."

"Well, you look beautiful."

"So do you." Rita fingered a strand of Marley's long chestnut hair. "When did you grow this out?"

"Ages ago. In fact, I was just thinking it was time for a change."

"I know where you can get a haircut real cheap." Rita wrinkled her nose. "Although it appears they cater more to old ladies these days."

"Your mom's salon?" Marley gave her a sympathetic look. "How's she doing anyway? I heard about her stroke. But Johnny said she's making great improvements."

Rita gave her an update as she perused a rack of sweaters. "Your shop is fabulous, Marley. I love it. So creative and well done. It looks like you."

"Thanks. It's been a fun project...a good distraction."

Rita was pretty sure Marley was referring to Rex, but she didn't want to push her. Not with their history. It was so good being with Marley again. No way was she going to jeopardize their friendship.

"How long are you in town?"

"I don't really know. But I let my manager know I wanted two weeks." Now Rita told Marley just how bad things were down in Hair and Now. "I don't even know if there's much I can do to help. But it needs help. That's for certain."

"Well, it probably didn't help that Zinnia opened her salon." Marley jerked her thumb over a shoulder. "Her place is right next door. Did you see it yet?"

"Not yet. But I wanted to take a peek. Unless that's rude." Rita considered this. "I don't want to step on her toes. But I would like to spy a little."

"It's pretty nice," Marley told her.

"I hear that Zinnia is pretty nice nowadays, too." Rita looked curiously at Marley.

"Oh, yeah." Marley nodded. "I remember how she used to be so snooty, like she thought she was so much older and cooler than us. But, really, she's changed a lot."

"I hear you're good friends with her."

"Good friends?" Marley's mouth twisted to one side as if she wasn't quite sure. "Who told you that?"

"Johnny. He gave me a ride from the airport. He made it sound like you and Zinnia were buddy-buddy—best friends."

"Well, we are friends, that's true. But best friends is a bit of a stretch. Maybe Johnny said that because he and Zinnia have been getting rather chummy."

Rita was surprised, but tried not to show it. "Interesting."

"Anyway, Zinnia is okay. Plus I've learned that it pays to be congenial with your business neighbors."

"Very smart." For some reason Rita felt relieved to know Zinnia hadn't replaced Rita as Marley's best friend. Not that Marley shouldn't have a new best friend. But hopefully someone a bit more reliable than Zinnia. Marley continued showing Rita around her shop, chattering happily and trying to catch up on the past ten years. But when customers came in, Rita felt guilty for distracting Marley from her customers.

"We should go to dinner or something," Rita said.

"Yes!" Marley exclaimed. "I can't do it tonight. But I have my high school girls working here on Saturday. I could do lunch." They exchanged phone numbers and worked out the details, then Rita continued on her way.

Zinnia's salon was impossible to miss. The windows were draped with bright-colored paper flowers—probably they were supposed to be zinnias. The zinnia motif continued inside the salon. Huge blossoms in canary yellow, bright orange, turquoise blue, and fuchsia went from floor to ceiling in a dizzying array. The chairs at the style stations and shampoo area were the same shades as the flowers, and everything else—the cutting stations, chairs, and floor—was all white. Very striking.

"May I help you?" a young woman with black hair tipped

with sky blue asked Rita, speaking loud to be heard above the music.

"I'm actually just looking, thanks." Rita made a stiff smile.

"*Looking?*" The woman's brow creased. "Oh, you mean for product." She pointed to a tall, well-stocked shelf behind her. "It's all right there."

Rita nodded as she moved toward the product display. "Yes. Thanks." As she stood there pretending to study the containers of what she knew was a less than stellar product line, she was actually peering through the open shelving into the relatively busy salon. At least it was busy compared to Hair and Now. It was bigger too, and although this salon had eight hair cutting stations, it clearly was not only about hair. Rita spied a large mani-pedi section, a makeup counter with three chairs, plus what appeared to be a tanning spray booth in back. Zinnia was certainly ambitious.

As Rita picked up a bottle of conditioner, still playing the shopper, she noticed Zinnia emerging from the back. If she hadn't known this was Zinnia's salon, she might not have even recognized her. Certainly, Zinnia was still petite and pretty in that pixie like way, but her hair, which used to be mousy brown and kinky, was now sleek and blond and long—very similar to how Rita wore her hair, but longer.

Zinnia's eyes grew wide as she spied Rita through the shelving unit, and before Rita could make a slick getaway, which seemed a bit immature, Zinnia had joined her. "Rita Jansen?" she said in disbelief. "My stars! Is that really you?"

"Hey, Zinnia." Rita made an uneasy smile. "I like your new do." She fingered a strand of Zinnia's hair, which felt in need of a good conditioning. "Looks good on you."

"Thanks." Zinnia made a puzzled expression. "Find what you're looking for?"

"Not exactly. This isn't my brand." Rita put the conditioner back on the shelf.

Zinnia's brows arched. "Really? What brand do you prefer?"

Rita continued being friendly, telling Zinnia about the new line her salon had started carrying. "But I think I might have enough to last me until I go back."

Now Zinnia expressed sympathy for Rita's mom. "Johnny told me all about it. Such a shame. I hope Donna's doing better."

Rita gave her a brief update. "But I'm not sure how long it'll be before she can return to work."

"Oh...that's too bad." Zinnia shook her head with pursed lips.

Rita waved her arm toward the wall. "This is really something, Zinnia. Very lively and cheerful."

Zinnia's green eyes twinkled. "You don't think it's too much?"

"Too much?" Rita feigned surprise. "I'm sure your clientele must love it."

"Oh, yeah, I get lots of compliments. My goal is for clients to leave here feeling happy and refreshed." She seemed to study a shiny white chair. "I think it accomplishes that."

"Well, you certainly seem busy enough." Rita nodded to a pair of women just entering the salon. "Good for you."

"Speaking of busy. One of those gals is my next appointment." Zinnia called out a warm greeting, then made what seemed a slightly forced smile for Rita. "Thanks for stopping in. I hope your mom gets well soon."

Rita felt relieved to get out of Zinnia's. She wasn't sure if it was the loud music or loud colors or simply the discomfort of spying. But she couldn't deny that Zinnia had a successful business on her hands, or that her clients seemed genuinely happy to be there. And despite the history Rita had with Zinnia, something she chose not to think about, she had to admit that her mom's competition was doing a lot right. As soon as she entered her mom's salon, she couldn't help but grimace over the severe contrast in these two salons. She would never say this to her mother, but Hair and Now felt like a mortuary compared to Zinnia's.

Chapter 6

"Why so glum, chum?" Charlene watched curiously as Rita stashed her handbag in the back room's closet. "Your mom still doing okay?"

"Oh, yeah. I mean, as far as I know."

"So what's troubling you?"

Rita slowly closed the closet door. "I was just at Zinnia's..."

Charlene scowled. "Oh...well, what did you think of it?"

"It's so different from here..."

"Yes, but didn't you find it, you know, a bit garish?"

Rita pursed her lips. "I'll admit it was on the bright side and a little loud for my taste. But it was friendly and upbeat."

"Looks to me like they had a paint-gun war in there and the flowers lost."

"Oh, I wouldn't go that far." Rita smiled at that image. "I mean, sure, I'm not a big fan of all those wild colors in one place, but it's not like we have room to talk." She waved her hands toward a dull rose-colored wall. "Have you really looked at this place lately, Charlene?"

Charlene shrugged. "Like I said, upgrades are expensive. We're hanging on by a thread as is. And now with Donna laid up. Well, I don't know..."

"I understand that. But I'm trying to think of some way—something not too pricey—to perk this place up."

"That would be nice." Charlene helped herself to another doughnut.

"I've seen some of those makeover shows. There are improvements you can do that aren't that costly. I just need to make a budget and see what I can do with it."

"Say..." Charlene held up a sugar coated finger. "I know a way we could make a little money... you know to use for your makeover plan... that is, if your mother would let us."

"What's that?"

Charlene took Rita over to the wall in the back. They called it Memory Lane, and it was full of old photos of the salon. "Remember *those*?"

"Yeah." Rita smiled at a cute shot of her mom. "Look at that wild mane of hair. That must've been the Farrah Fawcett era."

Charlene pointed to one of the earliest pictures. "No, I mean, look at this picture of the salon, taken when we first opened."

Rita looked at one of her mom in a haircutting chair. Hamming it up with a hand behind her head, she had a cheesy smile. "Mom's signature frosted shag haircut. Circa the mid-seventies. Mom said that's what everyone wanted when they came in here those early days."

"No, Rita, I mean, look at those chairs." Charlene tapped a green chair in the photo.

Rita bent forward, squinting to see the chairs better. "I don't really remember those chairs. But that's because Mom changed everything when I was pretty young."

"Well, did you know that we still have those green chairs?"

"Seriously?"

"Yes. Your dear mother has refused to let them go. At first she thought she might open a second salon and use them. Then she just forgot about them. But they're all in the there." She pointed to the door that led into the storage area that Rita remembered as a nightmarish sort of place that no one ever wanted to venture into.

"Oh...?" Rita frowned. "And...?"

"And according to my daughter-in-law, you can sell things like that on eBay and Craigslist. Some people are really into all that old stuff and will pay big money for them."

"Really? You think we could actually sell the chairs?"

"Sure. If you could get Donna to agree."

"Interesting idea..."

Charlene glanced at the clock on the wall. "Time for my three o'clock. Just a haircut, and we don't have any more appointments. Jillian and Yolanda already went home. I could stick around until closing in case there are walk-ins. That is unless you plan to be here."

"I'll be here," Rita told her. "Go ahead and take off when you finish."

"I'll put the towels in the washer before I leave, if you wouldn't mind putting them in the dryer."

"No problem." Rita opened the door to the storage room and turned on the lights.

"You're really going in there?" Charlene looked concerned.

"Yeah. If you don't hear from me before you leave, send in a search party."

Charlene laughed. "Will do."

The storage room was long and narrow. Like a man-made cave, it went the full length of the entire salon. And, of course, it was filled with everything imaginable and sometimes reminded Rita of a scene from a Stephen King movie. Bracing herself for spiderwebs and who knew what else, she started to create an alley past broken hairdryers, fake plants, shelving units, wobbly tables, boxes of Christmas decorations, rolled-up area rugs, cardboard boxes, and plastic crates. She had no idea what she'd do if the lights went out— probably scream for help.

About midway through she discovered a row of ghostly-looking lumps. Covered in old sheets, she suspected these were the chairs. She gingerly removed the first sheet to reveal it was indeed a chair. But it seemed to be a much brighter green than what she'd seen in the faded old photo. In fact, upon closer inspection, this chair was quite handsome. Constructed of stainless steel and covered in lime green vinyl, it wasn't only retro-cool, but as she sat down in it, she discovered it was quite comfortable, too.

"What a treasure!" she exclaimed as she attempted to move the chair into the alley she'd made. Because of the heavy metal base and solid construction, she could barely budge it, and there was no way she could carry it out of the storage room. Not about to give up, she transformed one of the area rugs into a skid, and after she maneuvered the chair onto the rug, she slowly slid it down the alley toward the door.

She was slightly breathless but excited when she finally got the lime green chair into the back room. It was really attractive and would probably look even better if it was dusted and cleaned up a bit. She grabbed a damp towel and some cleaning solution, and went to work on it. By the time she finished, she could imagine a very upscale LA salon being interested in something like this. And to think they had a full set! She went over to look at the old photo again. Not just haircutting chairs, but shampoo chairs, too. She sat down in the chair again, testing to see if it still turned and moved up and down. A little oil and it would probably be as good as new.

"Hey, look what you found." Charlene grinned as she came into the back room with a laundry basket of towels.

"These are really cool chairs." Rita stood up to admire it again.

"I think someone might pay good money for them." Charlene shoved the towels into the washer, pouring in soap.

"They seem really well made."

"Well, they didn't come cheap." Charlene turned on the machine then came over to examine the chair. "Not even back in the seventies. But Donna insisted on the best. And with the money that Bernice gave her to invest in this place, she could afford it." Charlene ran a hand over the smooth lime green vinyl. "Hair and Now was a happening place back in the seventies. We were hopping busy all the time. Kept all eight cutting chairs filled, with women in the waiting area." She sighed. "But that was then."

Rita returned to the old photos. "The salon was pretty cute," she said. "I really like those floors. Perfect with these chairs. I'm surprised Mom wanted to change everything. Especially with these chairs still in such great condition."

"Some of her clientele had made negative comments... thought the green was too bright. And business had been really booming, so your mom could afford to redecorate. Of course, dusty rose was all the rage at the time. The customers loved it... back then."

"But this color of green is so much more contemporary," Rita said. "In a retro-cool sort of way. And these chairs are so well made. It would be expensive to match this quality with something new."

"Your mom's always had a good eye for quality...when she could afford it." Charlene was pulling on her coat now. "Speaking of Donna, I thought I'd swing by and say hello to her on my way home."

"Tell her hi for me. And tell her I'm still here, trying to figure out how to make this place work better. That should make her happy."

"But I'm not going to mention the chairs." Charlene shook her head. "I'll leave that to you."

Charlene left and Rita sat back in the chair, wondering what she really could do to make this place work better...as well as make her mom happy. But she had a feeling the answer was going to be found in these lime green chairs. And not necessarily in selling them, either.

Rita was just sliding the fifth chair into the back room when she realized that someone was trying to get in through the back door. She glanced at the clock by the washing machine and, seeing it was well after seven and way past closing time, she got worried. Who would be coming here at this hour? Remembering what Charlene had said about local break-ins, she crouched down behind the chairs and tried to come up with an escape plan.

"I'll start up front and you start here in the back," a male voice announced as footsteps came into the room and the door closed.

"I *always* have to start in the back," another man said.

"That's because you're the younger brother."

"But it's *harder* work back here."

"I know." He chuckled. "Why do you think I want the front?"

"Hey, Mason, why are the lights on in here?"

"And what's up with those green chairs over by the bathroom?"

Peering between the chairs, Rita could see these guys had on red and white jackets with the words *Jolly Janitors* stitched on the fronts. So that was it.

"Oh, uh, hello," she said a bit sheepishly as she stood up. And now both men jumped back as if they were afraid of her. They were young African Americans and, based on their conversation, she assumed they were brothers.

"What're you doing here?" the taller guy pulled a phone from his pocket, holding it toward her like a weapon. "Should I be calling the police?"

"I'm Rita Jansen," she said quickly. "My mom is Donna Jansen, the owner."

"You supposed to be here?" the shorter guy asked with narrowed eyes.

"Yes." She nodded.

"Then why are you hiding like that?"

"I heard someone come in and thought you were burglars." She approached them, holding out her hand. "My apologies. I can see that you're simply with the janitorial service."

"Yeah. I'm Mason," the taller one said cautiously. "And this is my brother, Drew."

She shook both their hands. "But I thought this was Johnny's account," she said as she went to get her coat and handbag.

"You know Johnny?" Mason sounded relieved, but still looked slightly suspicious.

"Yes. I went to school with him."

"At JFK?" Drew asked with interest. "That's where we go. Mason's a senior. I'm a sophomore."

"You're in high school and you work for Jolly Janitors?"

"Just part time. It's how we're earning money for college," Mason explained.

"Well, good for you. And I have to say that everything seemed very clean and neat when I got here this morning. Jolly Janitors do good work." She pulled on her coat. "I'm going to get out of your way now. I assume you lock up and turn everything off?"

"That's right, ma'am," Drew assured her.

She told them goodbye then hurried out into the cold dark night. They seemed like nice guys, and it was probably a good job for earning college tuition. But as she drove through the parking lot, she wondered about Johnny. What kind of job was it for a man going on thirty?

Instead of going home like she'd planned, Rita decided to swing by the hospital. Visiting hours didn't end until eight. If she hurried she'd be able to spend the last fifteen or twenty minutes with her mom. Of course, when she got to her mom's room, she remembered that her dad would still be there, too.

"Since you're here, I think I'll go home," Richard quietly told her. "I still haven't had dinner and I'm a little worn out."

"Yes, yes," she eagerly said. "No problem." She waited as he bent down to whisper something in her mom's ear, watching as her mom's eyes lit up. Then he gently kissed her, squeezed her hand, and said goodbye.

"Sorry to interrupt," Rita told her mom as she went to her bedside. "But I was eager to talk to you tonight."

"Hah-lo," she said slowly.

"Hello to you, too." Rita said. "How are you doing?"

"Gooo..." Donna made a half smile.

"Glad to hear it." Now Rita began to tell her mom about finding the green chairs. "They're such cool chairs, Mom. I can't believe you kept them all these years. Charlene thinks they'd bring a good price on eBay or—"

"No." Donna held up her left hand. "No."

Rita patted her hand. "I know. Charlene also said you don't want to sell them. And I agree with you one hundred percent."

Donna's left eyebrow went up. "Yeah?"

"Yeah." Rita nodded. "The chairs are in fabulous shape, Mom. I sat in them and they're comfortable, too. I think we should put them back into Hair and Now. I think we should bring Hair and Now back to its former splendor. I was looking at the old photos in the back room. It was such a cool place, Mom. I never really saw it as a kid. At least not that I remember. But it would be a great-looking salon. Very uptown." She paused. "Am I talking too fast?"

"Nooo..."

"Do you like this idea, Mom?"

"Yeah..."

"Will you let me go ahead with it?"

Now Donna looked perplexed.

"Are you worried about money?"

"Yeah..."

"I have a little money to spare. I've been really good at saving. I want to invest some of it in your salon. I think it's a worthwhile investment."

Donna's left eyebrow arched again. "Yeah...?"

"Yeah." Rita nodded eagerly. "Please, let me do this, Mom. I've never been so excited about a project before. I think it'll be fun and exciting. Is it okay?"

Donna just looked at Rita now, as if trying to decide. "Yeah..." she finally said. "Gooo..."

Rita bent down to kiss her mom's cheek. "Great. You won't be sorry. And don't worry about a thing. I've already started putting together a plan."

Donna looked like she wanted to say something more. Probably to give some advice or some warning or ask a question. But finally she just let out a deep breath and gave Rita her funny little half smile.

Rita went to the salon again on Saturday morning. It was slightly busier than the previous day, but that wasn't saying much. And it was never so busy that anyone asked her to take an appointment. But that was fine with her. She spent most of the morning just measuring things, making notes, and doing research on the Internet. Then about an hour before she was supposed to meet Marley for lunch, she went down to Cabot's Upholstery Shop at the far end of the mall. Using her phone to show the proprietor the boxy-shaped waiting room chairs, she asked him how much it would cost to have them recovered.

"Depends on what you want them covered with." Mr. Cabot adjusted his glasses to peer more closely at the photos. "These chairs look pretty straightforward. How many are there?"

"Five. Not that we usually need them, but you never know." She quickly explained the Hair and Now situation, including her financial and timeline limitations.

"I heard about Donna's stroke." He shook his head. "Such a sweet woman. Too bad about that."

"I want her to be completely wowed by this makeover." Now she told him about the lime green chairs she planned to recycle. "So I want something that goes with that. It could be a solid in a similar shade, or maybe even a print." He excused himself to get some samples then returned with an interesting book of retro prints, including several with lime green. "I really love this one." She pointed to a bold green and white print that was reasonably priced.

He nodded, removing the piece from the ring so Rita could take it with her to help her make other decorating choices. "You need these when?"

"As soon as you can get them done."

He scratched his chin with a thoughtful expression. "Lucky for you it's a slow time of year. By the time the fabric gets here—you say five chairs?"

"That's right. But I'd settle for three."

"I could maybe get all five done by mid February."

She frowned.

"That's all five though. You could have the others as soon as they're finished. Maybe two or three in ten days."

She brightened and they shook on it. Mr. Cabot promised that someone would be down to pick them up in a few days. "Not all at once," he said as he wrote something down. "That way your folks will have something to sit on."

"Yes. That's a good idea."

With that settled, she went out to meet Marley for lunch at Noah's Ark.

"This is so fun," she told Marley as they settled into a booth. "Just like old times."

"I'm so glad we've buried the hatchet." Marley smiled.

"We should've done it a long time ago."

"Yeah, but we've both been busy with jobs...and life." Marley's eyes lit up. "Which reminds me, I forgot to ask you about your love life yesterday. I can't believe you're still single. What's up with that?"

Rita gave her a condensed report, explaining how her career took a lot of her time during the first few years and finally confessing how her skill at picking guys was challenged at best. "At first I thought it was the general shallowness of living in Beverly Hills, but the truth is I just consistently attract the wrong guys."

"You and me both."

"So...how are things with you and Rex?"

"Didn't Johnny tell you?"

"What?"

"We're separated. Just this fall."

"Oh...I'm sorry."

"I'm not." Marley's mouth puckered in a frown. "Okay, maybe that's not true. I mean, no one likes to fail at something. Especially a marriage. But the truth is I was holding on to our marriage these last few years out of nothing more than pure stubbornness. So many people predicted we'd never make it five years, let alone ten...I just wanted to prove them wrong."

"So it's been hard?"

"*Hard?* It's been sick and twisted and dysfunctional and painful...yeah, you could say it's been hard."

"I'm so sorry."

And now Marley unloaded her whole sad story on Rita, telling how Rex had started cheating shortly after their wedding. "For all I know he was cheating before that, too. I don't think he knows how not to cheat. It's like he's got WOMANIZER stamped onto his forehead, but only a certain kind of woman can read it. You know?"

"That's got to hurt."

"Yeah. I mean, I didn't really know about his affairs for the first few years. Looking back, I think I knew on some levels. A lot of little things felt off...and I often suspected something was wrong. You know what they say about twenty-twenty hindsight. But just the same, I was in total denial."

"That's not so unusual."

"When my parents helped me get my shop started—that was about four years ago—I got so caught up in setting everything up, getting inventory, and making it work that I sort of forgot about Rex." She made a pathetic laugh. "And, no doubt, he'd already forgotten about me." She leaned forward peering into Rita's eyes. "But you know what really sucks now?"

"What?"

"Rex doesn't want to divorce."

"You gotta be kidding."

"Nope. He swears he still loves me. But I know that's not true. You don't treat people you love the way he's treated me."

"Then why does he want to stay married?"

"I think he knows a good thing when he sees it. Secondhand Rose is making profits. I'm becoming independent for the first time in my life. His job doesn't pay that well...why not hang on to me, let me pay the bills, take care of everything at home, and he can keep running around with all his girlfriends? Nice, huh?"

Rita groaned. "That does suck."

"So...it'll be an interesting ride this year." She held up her hands. "But already I feel better. I like being free."

"Yeah...freedom is good." Yet even as she said this, Rita wasn't so sure she still believed it. Sometimes she really longed for a good man to love, a loyal man who would love her enough to partner with her for life. Kind of like how her parents had done. But for some reason it had escaped her.

Marley slowly shook her head. "Man, Rita, what was I thinking? Getting married when I was only twenty? I must've been certifiably crazy." She made a sheepish grin. "Oh, yeah, you tried to tell me that, didn't you?"

"Not in a very helpful way, unfortunately."

"That wasn't your fault. I wouldn't listen to anyone back then. Not even my best friend. I was so over the moon that Rex Prescott wanted me—little old me. And then I was head over heels about having the perfect wedding. It was like my fairy tale coming true. I thought for sure we would live happily ever after. What a fool."

"You know what they say...love is blind."

"So, seriously, you haven't fallen in love yet?"

"Not seriously. I mean, sure, I've put my heart out there a few times...been hurt a few times. But I wouldn't call it real love. Usually it's just because I trust a guy who turns out to be a jerk."

"And there's no one you're interested in right now? No one you'd like to get to know better? To date perhaps?"

Rita felt her cheeks grow warm as a certain unexpected name flashed through her mind—a certain *Jolly Janitor's* name. But there was no way she was going to say that name out loud. Not because Johnny was a janitor, she told herself, but simply because she knew it was ridiculous to get involved with someone in Chicago when she lived in Beverly Hills.

"Aha," Marley said triumphantly. "There *is* someone."

To distract her old friend, who used to see right through her, Rita told Marley a little about Dr. Wright.

"A doctor...hmm...that wouldn't be too bad."

"But I'm really not interested in him. Mostly I find it amusing."

"Amusing is a good place to start. Especially with a doctor."

"Yeah, I was teasing Mom the other day, saying she didn't have to have a stroke just for me to meet a doctor. I mean, really, that's taking it a little too far." They both laughed, making good-natured jokes about moms picking out future spouses.

And then, finally, after they'd talked for more than two hours, Marley announced she had to end the reunion and get back to the shop. "The girls will need a break by now. And I don't like having just one girl in the shop by herself."

They hugged and promised to stay in close touch, then parted ways. As Rita went back down to Hair and Now, she was already back to mentally planning the big changes she had in mind for the salon's renovation. She knew she'd need to go about the whole thing very carefully. She would keep their doors open as long as she possibly could because she knew the hairdressers' needed their income just as much as her mom did. But she also knew that she needed to move fast if she was going to accomplish this monumental task in less than two weeks—and that was her goal. Whether it was possible or practical or sensible remained to be seen. But, for the sake of her mom and her family, she was determined to give it her best shot.

Chapter 7

Rita wasn't surprised that the appointment book was blank after five o'clock for Saturday night. And she could tell that the hairdressers weren't too disappointed to go home early.

"Although we've been known to have a walk-in on a Saturday night occasionally," Charlene said as she buttoned her coat. "Some desperate young woman with a big date who can't get into Zinnia's."

"Well, I'll be here," Rita assured her. "Even if I'm in the back room, I'll hear the buzzer. Don't worry, I can handle it."

"And you know that Donna quit being open on Sundays a few years ago."

Rita nodded. "Right. But I might come over here and try to get some things done tomorrow anyway. I don't have much time to pull this thing off."

"So, I'll see you on Monday morning."

Rita locked the back door and continued her sorting and

moving program, which was quickly filling the back room with a lot of junk. Her plan was to thin that horrible storage room down so that it could become a usable space for her up-coming renovation project. She would borrow her dad's pickup on Monday to take boxes of throwaway and giveaway stuff out of here. Then she would continue cleaning and oiling the lime green chairs and store them in the cleaned-out space.

She was just stacking another cardboard box by the back door when she heard the buzzer ring. Was it possible she had a customer? When it was almost closing time? She frowned at her dirty hands and messy clothes. A client was a client. The least she could do was to get the woman comfortable then come back here and quickly clean herself up.

"Hello?" she called out as she hurried into the salon.

But instead of a woman, it was a man. Johnny Hollister was walking through the salon like he owned the place. Of course, she remembered, he cleaned the salon...it would only be natural he'd feel comfortable in here.

"Sorry to intrude," he said as they met in the middle.

"That's okay." She put her hands behind her back. "Isn't it a little early to clean? It's not quite closing time yet." Now she noticed that he was dressed in neat tan cords and a dark brown zippered sweater. "But you don't look like you're here to clean."

"No. I'm not working right now."

She studied his curly brown hair. "A haircut then?"

He grinned. "Think I need one?"

She frowned. "Not exactly...I mean, it looks fine at that length. Natural wave is great camouflage for an overdue hair-cut." She tipped her head slightly. "Although I suppose it could be cleaned up some around the sides and the back...if you liked."

He reached up and mussed it a little. "I don't know. I sort of like it a little long in winter. Keeps me warmer. To be honest, that's not why I'm here."

"Then why are you here?"

"To see how you're getting on."

"Oh." She nodded slowly. "I'm getting on just fine. Thanks." She moved to the nearby sink, where she quickly washed her hands.

"Ricky told me about what you're doing."

"He did?" She turned back around, drying her hands as she studied him again. Really, he was awfully nice looking . . . and well mannered too. A girl could do worse. "What did Ricky say?"

"That you're trying to help Donna by giving this place a makeover."

"Oh . . . well, that's true."

"Sounds like a big undertaking. I thought maybe you could use a hand with something."

"Seriously?" She blinked. "You came here to help me?"

"Why not?"

She pointed to his tidy clothes. "For one thing, you're dressed too nice." She tipped her head toward the back room. "I've got a serious mess going on back there." She told him about cleaning out the back room. "Decades' worth of garbage and crud and spiderwebs and dust. I even found a couple of skeletons."

"What?"

She laughed. "Halloween decorations."

"Oh." He nodded. "Yes. Donna does love to decorate for holidays."

"And she'll be happy to know that I'm not throwing her decorations out. Although I am sifting and sorting and clearly marking the crates so they'll be easy to find and use. But trust me, there's plenty of real garbage to toss. Mom's never been the most organized person, and she doesn't like getting rid of things."

"You're a good daughter, Rita."

Something about the way he said this, or maybe it was the warmth in those chocolate-brown eyes, enticed her to open up with some of the ideas she'd been noodling on these past few days. "Come on back and I'll show you what I've done," she said.

The first thing she showed him was the lime green chairs, explaining how they were the original ones for Hair and Now. "To be honest, these are my real inspiration. Everything I do will be to make them look great."

"Wow, these are very cool." He tested one, giving it a little turn. "Feels like this one might need a little oil and maintenance."

"They all do. I was thinking about asking my dad to help. He's pretty mechanical. Except that he's so overwhelmed with everything else right now. And I'd hate for him to come in here and see how it looks. He might not get it. He can be awfully protective of Mom. It's sweet, but it can get complicated, too. He'd be worried about the mess this could turn into."

"Sometimes you have to make a mess before you can really clean something up."

"Exactly." She nodded eagerly.

"I'm a little mechanical, too." He was down on his knees now, examining beneath. "It's a very simple construction style. But good and solid. I could probably get your chairs working properly."

"Could you, really? I'd be happy to pay you for your time and—"

"We can figure that out later." He stood, brushing the dust off his knees. "Those boxes by the door—are they trash?"

"That pile on the right is. The one on the left is for Good-will or something like that."

"I've got my pickup. How about if I pull around back and get them out of here for you tonight?"

"That would be awesome!"

"I'll be right back," he promised.

While he was gone, Rita dashed to the bathroom, where she did a quick fix-up on her hair and makeup. Going to this trouble for a man she wasn't really interested in seemed a bit silly, but she decided to simply chalk it up to her personal vanity. She came out of the bathroom and was surprised to find him already picking up one of the trash boxes.

"I have a key," he explained. "Remember?"

"Oh, yeah." She nodded, hurrying over to pick up a box herself, following him outside and watching as he slid the box into the back of a shiny red pickup.

"Let me take that." He reached for her box. "And if you're going to help with this, you better get your coat on."

She got her coat and together they loaded not only the trash boxes but the giveaway stuff as well, completely filling the back of his pickup. As he closed the gate, Johnny assured her that Jolly Janitors was used to dealing with this sort of thing. "We have lots of great organizations we donate reusable goods to."

"You have no idea how much I appreciate this," she said as they hurried back into the warmth of the back room. "You are a godsend."

"Now I'll tell you why I really stopped by," he said as he washed his hands in the laundry sink. "I wanted to see if you needed to grab a bite to eat."

"Come to think of it, I'm starving," she admitted. "But I'll only go if you let me treat."

"Let *you* treat?" He looked slightly confused as he dried his hands.

"To thank you for your help tonight," she insisted.

"But I don't think I can—"

"That's my final offer," she told him. "Either I treat or I don't go. Take it or leave it."

He held up his hands. "I'll take it."

"Where do you want to go?" she asked as she reached for her handbag.

"Oh...I don't know." He looked uncertain. "We could just go up to Noah's Ark."

"Sounds great." She didn't admit to him that she'd eaten lunch there already today. Hopefully Noah would be gone by now. They went through the front, turning off the lights and going outside. "I keep forgetting to ask someone what they're doing out here." She waved her hand toward the construction mess in the courtyard. "It's such a disaster area—I'm sure it can't be helping the businesses down here."

"You haven't heard?" Johnny locked the door for her. "They're putting the ice rink back in."

"No kidding?" She looked at the mess with more appreciation now. "That's great."

"Yeah. And the new owners are great people. It'll be called On Ice, and there will be a snack bar for kids as well as an upscale rinkside restaurant catering to the older crowd."

"That sounds lovely. When is it supposed to be finished?"

"It's further along than it looks. They wanted it done before Valentine's Day. They're planning a big grand opening celebration with ice sculptures and skating and all sorts of things."

"That's perfect!" she exclaimed. "I should have Hair and Now all renovated and hopefully doing good business by then, too. What great timing." As they rode up the escalator she told him about some of the promotion ideas she had for the salon.

"So you'll still be here by the time On Ice opens?" he asked as they strolled down the busy mall.

She considered this. "I told my manager two weeks. My first week is up on Monday. It'll be two weeks on February eighth, although I haven't booked my return flight yet."

"That's only about nine days. You sure you can get Hair and Now renovated that quickly?"

"Actually, I'm not sure. I'm a little worried. I've worked out a schedule, but it's cutting it pretty close. If anything goes wrong, I'll be up a creek."

"Why not ask for a third week?" he suggested. "It would be a shame to leave without completing what you started."

She nodded. "I know. It would break my heart to have Mom show up to her salon only to discover that it's half finished."

He pushed open the door to the café, waiting as she went in ahead of him. Johnny got high marks for good manners. Rita remembered the handsome attorney Margot had set her up with last summer. Alistair may have had an impressive job and a flashy car, but he'd been a self-centered snob who was clueless about women, and it only took one date to figure that out.

To her surprise, Noah's Ark was different in the evenings. Instead of ordering at the counter, they were seated at a table, which not only had a tablecloth but a votive candle as well. A young woman set down ice waters, handed them menus, and told them tonight's specials.

"This doesn't feel like Noah's Ark to me," she whispered after the waitress left.

"You haven't been here for dinner?"

"Not in years."

"They try to cater to a different crowd in the evenings now. As you may have noticed this mall's a little short on restaurants these days. Besides the food court and the steakhouse, this is pretty much it for dinner."

"That should be good news for the ice rink restaurant." She studied the menu, relieved that it was relatively simple. Especially since she was slightly rattled by the fact that this was feeling strangely like a date.

"The lasagna is killer," he told her. "If you're hungry, that is."

"I liked the sound of the seafood pasta the waitress mentioned." Rita set her menu down, and while Johnny was studying his, she studied him. She wondered how she would feel about him if they were sitting in a Beverly Hills restaurant right now. Was her hesitation over Johnny because of the distance—or because of his occupation? She honestly didn't believe it was the latter. Because the truth was—she *was* interested. Just guarded. But then she was usually guarded when it came to guys. Even so it bothered her that she felt guarded with Johnny. That made no sense. Really, was she so shallow that she'd allow his line of work to come between them? Was that what came from living in Beverly Hills? When had she become that snooty? After all, in a lot of people's eyes, she was "only a hairdresser," the daughter of a hairdresser.

As she sipped her water, she made up her mind. She was no longer going to think of Johnny as a Jolly Janitor. She was going to accept him for the good person she knew that he was—Johnny Hollister, a man who wasn't too proud to take out her trash. She smiled with relief.

"You look happy," he said as he set his menu down.

"I am happy." She truly was.

"Any special reason?"

Her smile got bigger. "I was just thinking how fun it's been getting to know you again. You're really a nice guy, Johnny."

He grinned back at her. "I was thinking the same thing about you, Rita."

Now, because her renovation project was so fresh on her mind, she started to run some of her ideas past him—asking his opinion and explaining how she planned to do the renovations in stages. He was surprisingly interested and full of helpful suggestions about where to find things at the best prices. As they were finishing up their dinner, he pulled out a small notepad and actually wrote down the names of several businesses that he'd recommended, handing them to her.

"But it sounds like you're going to need some hands-on help too," he told her. "Painting those tall walls, installing the new flooring, getting old stuff ripped out and new stuff installed, and trying to do it quickly enough not to lose business...could be a challenge."

"Ricky offered to help," she told him.

"But his back and leg...?"

"I know." She sighed. "I'm not really sure how much help he could be. I asked the hairdressers, but...well, besides Charlene, they didn't sound too enthused."

"I know a couple of guys who could help out," he said suddenly. "A pair of brothers who're still in high school and—"

"Mason and Drew?" she asked curiously.

"That's right. Did you meet them at the salon?"

She explained how they took her by surprise. "I, uh, actually thought that you said that was your account. I expected to see you coming to clean it."

He pressed his lips together, nodding slowly. "Yeah...well, we sometimes switch things around. Keeps it interesting, you know?"

"Oh...right. Well, anyway, they do good work. In fact, the only thing I can't complain about in regard to Hair and Now is the cleanliness. It might be worn and outdated and have practically no customers, but it is very clean." She laughed.

"Anyway, I think we could get Mason and Drew to help out. They're hard workers and available for weekends and evenings."

"I can pay them a little something." Rita knew she'd have to budget in some help or risk not getting it done.

"We can figure that out later." He put his notepad away then glanced up in surprise. "Looks like we've got company," he said quietly.

Rita looked up in time to see Marley and Zinnia coming straight for their table.

"Well, hello there," Zinnia said in a ultra-friendly tone. "Did you guys have dinner already?"

"We did," Johnny confirmed.

"And it was delicious," Rita added.

"We came over for dessert and coffee." Zinnia put a familiar hand on Johnny's shoulder. "You know how good their berry cobbler à la mode is."

"But we don't want to intrude," Marley said quickly, eyeing Rita curiously.

"No, of course not. Besides there's no place to sit." Zinnia looked around the restaurant and made a sad face. "So I guess we'll have to go somewhere else, Mar."

There was a long, uneasy pause, and Rita was about to say something, but Johnny beat her to the punch. "Why don't you join us?" Johnny stood, politely pulling out chairs for Marley and Zinnia.

"But we don't want to interrupt your *date*," Zinnia said with a questioning look. "I *assume* this is a date."

"No, no," Rita assured her. "It's not a date. More like a business dinner. Johnny is helping me with something— uh—a project." She tossed him a warning look, hoping he'd take the hint and not mention their prior conversation to Zinnia.

"That's right," Johnny told the other women. "Rita was cleaning out a storage room and I was taking out the trash for her. Just part of Jolly Janitors' customer satisfaction service."

"Yes. And I offered to treat him to dinner as a thank-you," Rita finished. "That's all. I had no idea that Noah's Ark had turned into such a swanky dinner place."

As they all chatted and made decisions on desserts, Rita couldn't help but notice how friendly and cozy Zinnia seemed to be with Johnny. As if they were dear old friends. Or perhaps something even more. Rita glanced at Marley, curious as to whether she had observed this, too. But Marley seemed to be simply taking it in stride.

"And don't forget that you still owe me for that bet," Zinnia was saying to Johnny. "I knew the Bulls were going down last week, but did you believe me?"

"That's because I never bet against my Bulls."

"Just the same, you owe me, Johnny Boy, and I'll be collecting." She ran a well-manicured finger down on his cheek, giggling. "You better watch out for me."

Unless it was Rita's imagination, Johnny was blushing. And despite all resolve, Rita was seeing red. And her anger wasn't directed at Johnny. Still, she reminded herself, this was *not* a date. She had said as much herself, hadn't she? Even so, she hurried to shovel down her tasty crème brûlée, finally making the excuse that she'd promised her dad and brother that she wouldn't be home late tonight. "I'll just run up and take care of the bill," she told Johnny in a formal way. "Thanks for helping me with the trash." She smiled at Zinnia and Marley. "See you girls around."

It wasn't until she was driving home, still feeling unreasonably flustered, that she realized that she hadn't only paid the bill for her dinner with Johnny, but she'd covered everyone else's confections and coffee, too. Well, maybe buying everyone dessert was what one got for allowing jealousy to creep into what had otherwise been a lovely evening. Maybe it was her just desserts.

Chapter 8

Rita offered to visit her mom early on Sunday morning. Based on what Ricky and her dad had told her Saturday night, her mom had made great strides in rehab the past few days. But perhaps Rita's hopes had been too high... because when she actually sat down with Donna, she was dismayed that she didn't seem to have progressed much further than the last time she'd seen her. Even so, Rita kept a positive smile on her face and bit her tongue as she waited for her mom to communicate her recent happenings via a few words, pantomime, and the drawing pad. Rita wished she had more patience, but finally she just had to tell her about some of the ideas for the salon.

Rita explained how she wanted to do a complete renovation to the salon, not only reusing the chairs, but putting in new floors and painting the walls and all sorts of things. She pulled out the fabric sample, laying it on the bed. "But I want it to be something you'll like. And it has to be done on a pretty tight budget." She shared some of her money-saving ideas and how she planned to do most of the labor herself. "Those lime green chairs are a real treasure," she reminded her. "You were so smart to hold on to them."

Donna nodded happily. "Yeah...yeah..."

"They'll make the salon really retro and chic. Like something you'd see in Beverly Hills. And I know I can do it, Mom. I just need your blessing for all the changes. I mean, it's not going to look the same at all. The pink will be totally gone."

"Yeah...yeah...yeah." Donna nodded, making her funny little half smile. "Yeah."

"Great." Rita bent down to hug her. "That's what I'm going to do then. And that means I can't be with you throughout the day as often as I have. Are you okay with that?"

"Yeah."

"Ricky will be home with you in the daytime. And then Dad gets home after work. And I'll see you when I can. But mostly I'll devote my time to redoing Hair and Now. I only have a couple of weeks to get it done." She still hadn't decided about extending her visit, but knew it made sense. "My goal is to have it finished before On Ice opens. I want to do some promotions in tandem with that. Does that sound good?"

"Yeah." Donna smiled. "Gooo...I like..."

Rita kissed Donna's cheek. "Well, I've got a full list today. Dad should be here any minute. But I'll be with you when you're at home tomorrow. I bet you'll be glad to get discharged."

Her mom's last "yeah" echoed in Rita's ear as she rode down the elevator. Clearly, Donna was as worn out from being in the hospital as her family was from visiting her there. Another reminder that Rita should do some homecoming preparations for her. So much to do. So little time. But at least she'd have a whole day without interruptions. Her plan was to finish cleaning all the lime green chairs, store them in the cleaned-out storage room, and then start stripping down areas of the salon that no one would miss, getting it ready for the big renovations she was planning for the end of the week. She'd have to close the shop from Saturday through Tuesday, which would give her four days to get it all done. Was that even possible?

Out in the hospital parking lot, she called Roberto's and punched in her manager's extension number. She knew that Vivienne wouldn't be there at this early hour on a Sunday, but maybe that was for the best. She left a long message, explaining about what she was doing and why and finally asking for an extra week. "I know this can't be considered vacation time," she said, even though she knew she hadn't taken two weeks of vacation every year. "But it's going to take that long to get my mom's salon set up . . . to do it right." She said a few more things, then promised to call back on Monday to confirm this was okay.

As she drove to Millersburg Mall, she felt confident that Vivienne would allow her an extra week. Vivienne had a reputation for being a hard-nosed businesswoman, but Rita knew she had a heart of gold. But Rita also knew that there were plenty of hairdressers who would gladly take her job if they could. Working at Roberto's of Beverly Hills was something she did not take for granted. She wanted Vivienne to know that.

Rita went right to work at the salon. She had her to-do list broken down by days, and before this day was over, she wanted to have everything on today's done and the salon ready for tomorrow's appointments. She was just taking down some old headshot photos, ones her mom had let her put up more than ten years ago, when she heard someone knocking on the front door. Tempted to ignore it since they were closed, Rita set the framed print on the floor. But when the knocking continued, Rita went to see.

"Marley," she said as she unlocked it. "What're you doing here?"

"I tried your cell phone," Marley told her. "But when you didn't answer, I figured I'd see if you were here. What's up?"

Rita updated her on the renovation project. "But I'd appreciate it if you kept all this under your hat."

"You mean don't tell Zinnia?"

Rita shrugged. "Yeah...I guess. I don't know why. Maybe I want it to be a surprise."

"Or maybe you want to keep the competition at bay."

Rita smiled. "Maybe..."

"Want to grab a bite?" Marley asked. "Or did you already have lunch?"

Rita sighed to see that it was nearly two, confessing she hadn't had anything since a carton of yogurt this morning. And so, once again, they headed for Noah's Ark, and, with a big bowl of Hungarian mushroom soup in hand, Rita led the way to a table under the rainbow.

"Why did you run off last night?" Marley asked as they ate their soups.

Rita shrugged as she broke a piece of sourdough bread. "Time to go?"

"Really?" Marley looked skeptical.

"It was late."

"Come on." Marley narrowed her eyes. "This is me, Rita. I *know* you."

"What are you saying?"

"You're into Johnny, aren't you?"

"No. Of course, not. He was helping me take out the trash, that's all. I wanted to repay him with dinner. Nothing more."

"Really...?" Marley still looked seriously doubtful.

"Oh, I don't know. What are you getting at, anyway?"

"I saw you and Johnny talking before we crashed in on you last night."

"Yeah...so...?"

"So, it looked like you guys were really into each other. Like some kind of mutual attraction was going on."

"Oh...?"

"Come on, admit it."

"Oh, Marley."

"Did you know that Zinnia has been pursuing Johnny for a couple of years now?"

"Seriously?"

"Absolutely." Marley nodded as she ate a bite of soup. "Take it from me. Zinnia is out to get him. She's got a whole big plan laid out. She's told me about it."

"Really?" Rita frowned. "Does Johnny like her?"

"He's always polite to her. But then Johnny is polite to everyone."

"Well, that makes sense in his business. You don't want to make enemies with the businesses you clean."

"Maybe so. But Johnny is a great guy, Rita. And if he's interested in you, why not—"

"It was just business, Marley."

"Okay..." Marley looked unconvinced. "So I suppose you're not interested in what Zinnia told Johnny about you last night."

"What do you mean?" Rita set down her spoon.

"Well, it's partly my fault."

"What are you talking about?"

Marley made a nervous smile. "Zinnia was asking me about you last night, when she invited me to go have dessert. Seems you piqued her curiosity after you'd gone spying in her salon."

"Really?"

"Yeah. For some reason she was extremely interested."

"And?"

"So I sort of told her about Dr. Wright."

"What?" Rita frowned. "Why would you—"

"Because Zinnia was acting like you were such a loser. She was putting down your mom's salon and acting like you really didn't work in Beverly Hills, acting like you'd come home because you couldn't make it there. And she made a point of you being single and never married, like you couldn't get a guy."

"What does that have to do with—"

"I know it was stupid. But I was bragging to her about how you had this doctor trying to get you to go out, making it into a bigger deal than it probably is."

"Oh..." Rita just shook her head, trying to figure this whole thing out.

"After you left, Zinnia started talking about Dr. Wright and you to Johnny and—"

"She what?" Now Rita was mad.

"Yeah. She made it sound like you and the good doctor were practically engaged and—"

"You've gotta be kidding!"

"I'm sorry, Rita. I tried to do damage control, but Zinnia just made me sound silly."

"I thought you said she'd changed." Rita shook her spoon at Marley.

"Well, she's changed some...but not completely...apparently. Maybe her true colors come out when you cross her. And I'm guessing that seeing you with Johnny last night felt like you'd crossed her, Rita. She's got you in her sights."

"Good grief!"

Marley put her hand on Rita's hand. "Will you forgive me?"

Rita let out an exasperated sigh. "Are you going to tell Zinnia about the makeover I'm giving Mom's salon?"

"No, of course not."

"If you keep that promise, I'll forgive you." Rita smiled. "And I'd forgive you anyway."

"You have my word, I won't tell her a thing about Hair and Now. And I'm sorry about the Dr. Wright slip of the lip."

"It doesn't matter." Rita dipped her spoon back in the soup and sighed. "Like I said, it was just a business dinner."

On Monday morning, Rita did some housekeeping, including giving her parents' bedroom a good deep cleaning. Then she made a quick run to the store to get some fruit and vegetables as well as a selection of soft and liquid foods that her mother could eat. She also picked up a balloon bouquet and some crepe paper then hurried home to make a welcome-home banner and make the house look festive.

By the time Richard and Ricky brought Donna home in the afternoon, she was almost too tired to appreciate much. But as Rita helped her into her bed, she muttered a barely intelligible. "Than' you."

"You're welcome, Mom." Rita kissed her cheek as she pulled the covers up to her chin. "Have a rest and we'll talk more later, okay?"

"Wai..." Donna held up her left hand like a stop sign.

"What?"

"Wai...don...go."

Rita paused to process this. "You want me to stay?"

"Yeah." Her mom nodded with one arched brow.

"You want to tell me something?"

"Yeah." Her mom reached up and tugged her hair.

"Hair?"

"Yeah." Now she made a scissors motion. "How...?"

"How is Hair and Now?"

"Yeah." She nodded eagerly. "How?"

So Rita gave her a quick update, even sharing about how Johnny helped her to haul out some trash, quickly explaining it really was trash and how she'd gone through everything. "I stored everything you want to keep in plastic cartons that are clearly marked." She told her about how great the storage room looked now. "And I'm keeping all the lime green chairs in there. They're mostly cleaned up and—"

"Wai..." Donna held up her left hand again.

"What?" Rita peered closely at her.

"You...go...hair..." Donna nodded.

"You want me to go to Hair and Now? Now?"

"Yeah."

"To keep working on it?"

"Yeah."

Rita smiled. "Well, I'd like to keep on it, Mom. But I promised Dad and Ricky to be here for you and—"

"Wai..." Donna reached for her tablet and after a bit, she drew stick figures of two men and one woman in a house. Then she clumsily wrote their names.

"You think Dad and Ricky can take care of you here. Meanwhile I'll keep the renovations going at Hair and Now?"

"Yeah." Donna looked relieved.

"Okay, Mom." Rita squeezed her hand. "I'll let the guys know."

"Than...you..."

Rita took Donna's writing pad out to show her dad and Ricky. She explained her mother's wishes. "I know she's worried about Hair and Now," she told them. "And rightly so. There's a lot to be done there to get that place back into a profitable business."

"And you really think you can do that?" Richard asked.

"I believe I can. But my time here is limited. I have to make the most of it. Mom seems to understand this."

"Then you should give it all you've got, Rita." Her dad made a hopeful smile. "It would be wonderful if your mother could go back to work...someday...but even if she can't, anything you can do to make Hair and Now work better will be appreciated."

"Maybe I can come over and help too," Ricky suggested. "You know, when Dad's here in the evenings."

"Great." Rita nodded. "There's not much you can do yet, but by the end of this week...into the weekend. How are you at painting?"

He shrugged. "I'll give it my best."

"That's all I can ask for."

As Rita drove her mom's car over to the mall, she couldn't help but feel relieved. As if she'd dodged a bullet. Cleaning a nasty storage room and reinventing an outdated hair salon was one thing; playing nursemaid was another. Although she would do it for her mother. For the time being she was thankful to let the men play the caretakers.

Chapter 9

Rita was surprised to see that all three beauticians had clients in their chairs. All three patrons were elderly, and the middle-aged woman in the waiting area explained that they were from a nearby retirement home. "Do you mind if I ask what made them choose Hair and Now?" Rita said to the woman.

The woman looked slightly uncomfortable. "The truth?"

"Please, I'd like to know."

"Well, the location is handy, but more than that this place never seems very busy. It's nice that I can bring three at once, even on short notice. That saves me some time."

"Thank you for your honesty." Rita smiled. "So if this place was more busy, but we were still able to handle three of your ladies at once, would you still bring clients to us?"

"Sure, why not." She held up her hand. "And another thing. I like that you're on the lower level and that Donna lets us park in back and use the back entrance."

"Good to know."

"Do you plan on becoming busier in the future?" The woman frowned at the salon as if she had her doubts.

"I'm doing some renovations and marketing that I hope will bring in new patrons. But even if we do get busier, I'd like to accommodate your ladies. Maybe we could have a senior day with discounts. Maybe offer treats and make it a fun social time."

"That sounds great."

Rita wrote this down in the idea section of her notebook. Then she turned back to today's list and remembered her promise to call Vivienne at Roberto's.

"We miss you around here," Vivienne said after Rita gave her the update on her mom's condition. "But I understand your desire to help with your mother's little salon and you can take that third week, although your vacation time will be used up at two weeks."

"Thanks, Vivienne. I appreciate it." Now Rita told her about the lime green chairs. "They're so cute. I can wait to see how the whole thing turns out."

"Send us photos," Vivienne said. "Before and after."

"Good idea."

"Hey, while I have you on the line, are you interested in our discontinued line of PBG product?"

Rita looked at the shelf she'd recently emptied. "We desperately need product and I love PBG, but we can't really afford it—not with all the other expenses of renovating."

"Can you afford to cover the postage?"

"Seriously?"

"Yes. If you pay shipping, you can have it all."

"Oh, Vivienne. That would be fabulous."

"Great. It's just taking up space in the storeroom. Email

me your shipping address and we'll get it out of here by tomorrow."

Next Rita called Aubrey, giving her the latest updates on
her mom and the news that she was extending her visit by
another week. And then, since Aubrey was being chatty, Rita
decided to mention a certain janitor. "He works for a company called Jolly Janitors. Can you believe it?"

"Kind of like Merry Maids?"

Rita laughed. "I guess . . ."

"So . . . you're having a little romance then," Aubrey said
with interest.

"No, it's not a romance. I'm just saying he's kind of interesting. I can't even imagine what Margot would say about it.
By the way, please don't tell her."

Aubrey just laughed. "Sure, it's okay for Margot to tease
me about my plumber guy, but you're going to keep your
Jolly Janitor under wraps."

"That's right."

"Fine. But I say if he's a nice guy, go for it. You're way
overdue for a nice guy, Rita."

Now Rita wished she hadn't said anything. What was she
thinking? "I can't really go for it, Aubrey. I've got work to do
here, and then it'll be time to get back there. No time for romance."

"Maybe you could bring your Jolly Janitor back here with
you. Maxwell has been talking about hiring an assistant. That
might be a step up for Johnny." She giggled. "Johnny . . . such
a cute name."

As much as Rita loved Aubrey, she really wished she'd kept
her mouth closed about Johnny. For some reason it felt wrong
to talk about him like this—and very juvenile. "Tell Margot
hi for me," she said before they hung up.

For the rest of the afternoon, Rita focused on the computer. She'd already downloaded a user-friendly program that should streamline the paperwork for everyone, but she wanted to familiarize herself with it enough to teach the others how to use it. And when the salon was empty of customers, she locked the front door and called an impromptu staff meeting.

First she gave them a quick introductory computer class. "It's super easy," she told them. "And until there's enough business to require a receptionist, it will be a real time saver for everyone." She also told them about the week's upcoming schedule and how they would be closed for business from Saturday through Tuesday. "I've already rescheduled what few appointments we had. And if you guys want to help out, with painting or cleaning or whatever, that would be great. I can only pay minimum wage, but I can have pizza delivered." Charlene promised to help out during the weekend and, to Rita's surprise, both Yolanda and Jillian volunteered to come in on Monday and Tuesday. Finally, she told them about some of the promotions she was planning, including a grand reopening that would coincide with the reopening of the ice-skating rink. "Just in time for Valentine's Day," she said. "If all goes well anyway."

Rita felt hopeful as her mom's employees left at five o'clock. They'd all seemed happy about the upcoming changes, showing more enthusiasm than she thought they were capable of. As usual, she planned to keep the salon open until the usual closing time. But she used this time to clean out the cutting stations that hadn't been needed in recent years, and finally, as she was taping a sign on the front window announcing the dates they'd be closed for renovations, a customer walked in.

"Dr. Wright?" She set the Scotch tape on the reception

desk and stared at him in wonder. "What're you doing here?" A wave of panic rushed through her. "Is something wrong with my mom?"

"No, no—not that I know of anyway. I thought she was discharged today."

"She was." Rita pushed a strand of hair away from her face. He smiled. "So, how is she doing?"

"She's fine...as far as I know. She was glad to get home...but tired." Rita peered curiously at him. "Did you come in for a haircut?"

"As a matter of fact, I probably could use one, don't you think?"

She studied his dishwater blond hair. It did look like it could use some help. "I suppose so."

"Do you have time?"

She glanced at her watch. "Well, we close at seven. But I could probably finish you up by then."

"Great." He removed his parka. And Rita, feeling a bit awkward, led him over to the shampoo station. Something about this felt slightly off, but what could she do?

"I'll warn you, men's cuts are not my specialty," she said as she vigorously scrubbed his head.

"I trust you."

Before long, he was seated at her mom's cutting station, and she was combing and snipping and eventually pulling out the clippers to clean up the collar line. Finally, she brushed the hair away from his neck, whipped off the cape, and proclaimed, "Voilà!"

He looked in the mirror and smiled. "Very nice. Thank you."

She was just removing a missed clipping of hair from his shoulder when she heard the door opening again. "We're closed," she called out as she turned around. But there, to her stunned surprise, was Johnny. Dressed in his red and white janitor jacket and blue jeans, he looked as if he was here to clean up. But why hadn't he come in through the back door?

"Sorry to intrude." His brow creased as he stood in the reception area. "But I'm not here for a haircut."

"Sorry. Come on in, Johnny." She made a nervous smile. "I just finished up with Dr. Wright and I was about to close shop."

"Not until I settle up with you." Dr. Wright pulled out his wallet. "And not until you stop calling me Dr. Wright, Rita. I have a first name, you know." He handed her his credit card.

"I see that you do." She read his name from the card as if she didn't already know it. "Winston D. Wright." As she went to the register she casually introduced the two men, explaining to Johnny that Winston had been one of her mom's physicians at Jackson Park. "But Mom went home today," she told Johnny. "And Dr. Wright—I mean *Winston*—came in for a haircut." Feeling a bit silly for overexplaining, she handed Winston his receipt. She waited for him to sign and tried not to frown at what seemed a slightly miserly tip, considering how she'd stayed open late for him. But she simply thanked him and walked him to the door.

"I wanted to ask you—"

"Closing time," she cheerfully interrupted him, jingling her keys as she handed him his jacket and opened the door. "Sorry to throw you out, but rules are rules."

Winston frowned, jerking his thumb to where Johnny was still leaning against the reception desk. "What about him?"

"Oh, Johnny?" She shrugged. "He's with our cleaning service. Jolly Janitors."

"*Jolly* Janitors?" Winston chuckled. "Do they tell jokes while they mop? Or whistle while they work?"

"Sometimes we do," Johnny responded good-naturedly.

"See you around, Winston." Rita gently put her hand on his shoulder, guiding the slightly bewildered man out the door, before she closed and locked it.

"Didn't mean to scare the good doctor away," Johnny said.

Rita went to the cutting station and picking up the broom began to sweep the hair from the floor. "You didn't scare him away. It was time for him to go."

He took the broom from her. "Why not let Jolly Janitors sweep your troubles away." And now he started to whistle as he swept.

She couldn't help but laugh as she sat down at the cutting station across from him. "Why didn't you use the back door?" she asked. "I mean, if you're here to clean, although it seems a little early."

"I'm not here to clean." He swept the hair into the dustbin and frowned down at it. "Your doctor friend has some gray hairs."

She chuckled. "I noticed."

He dumped the hair into the trash then turned to look at her. "Is it a serious relationship?"

"Me and Dr. Wright?" She gave him a funny look.

"Don't you mean *Winston?*"

"Yes . . . Winston. And, no, it is not a serious relationship. I couldn't have been more surprised when he showed up just now."

"But you gave him a haircut?"

She stood and shrugged. "This is a hair salon, Johnny. It's what we do."

"But it was closing time."

"Not quite." She cleaned the scissors and dropped the comb into the sterile solution. "And I can't really afford to turn away business." She tipped her head to one side. "So, if you're not here to clean, why are you here?"

"I stopped by to let you know that Mason and Drew want to help with your renovations. I just need to let them know when exactly."

She told him her plans and how she'd extended her visit a week. "But I'd really like to get it totally wrapped up by next Tuesday. That will give us a couple of days to get up to speed. And I'm getting postcards to send out to our list of clientele, inviting them to stop by for a sneak peek and goodies on Friday afternoon. Plus, I've bought ad space, announcing the grand reopening on Valentine's Day weekend."

"Sounds like a good plan." He looked around the salon. "And assuming you're not changing anything as far as electric and plumbing goes, it should be doable."

"Yes, the cutting stations and shampoo area will all be in the same places."

"I was curious as to whether you've got the tools you'll need. You know, things like drills and hammers and paintbrushes and ladders and drop cloths. That can all add up when you're trying to stay on budget."

"My dad has a few things I can probably use, but he's not really much of a tool guy. I mean, besides the automotive stuff. He's not a real handyman."

"That's the other reason I stopped by. I thought you might want to borrow a few things."

"Really? You've got those kinds of tools? That you can lend me?"

He nodded. "And I have the evening off if you'd like to go pick some things out. Then I can bring them over here on

Friday night—to be sure that it's all ready for your team on Saturday."

"That'd be fabulous."

"How about if I drive around back while you lock up?"

Rita rushed around turning off lights and throwing wet towels from the washer into the dryer, and even taking time to retouch her hair and makeup. She was just pulling on her coat when Johnny came in. "Ready to rock and roll?" he asked as he led her out to his pickup.

"This is so generous of you," she said as he opened the door, letting her in.

"Do you mind if we pick up some takeout food?" he asked as he got behind the wheel. "I haven't eaten since noon."

"Sounds lovely."

"I'm craving a cheeseburger and shake, but I'm guessing you might be one of those California cuisine girls, so we—"

"I would adore a cheeseburger and shake," she confessed.

"I know just the place."

Within minutes, loaded down with their to-go dinner, Johnny was unlocking the door to what appeared to be some kind of warehouse. "Where are we?" she asked curiously as he led them in, flipping on lights.

"Jolly Janitors," he said.

"Oh..." She looked around the large, organized space. "Nice."

"We can eat in the office." He led her over to a room with windows, unlocking the door and turning on lights. "Warmer in here."

"They give you keys to the office?" She set the bag containing their shakes on what looked like a conference table.

He chuckled as he opened a nearby cabinet, extracting a couple of paper plates and setting them across from each other on the table. "Take off your coat and make yourself at home."

"You won't get in trouble for doing this?" She set the shakes by the paper plates.

"Nah. It's okay." He hung his red and white janitor jacket over the back of chair and flipped on a switch that instantly produced music—not too loud, but nice.

"You're sure?" She looked nervously around, taking in the sleek dark wood cabinets, the big, tidy desk with its comfy looking leather chair. What if Johnny's boss walked in on them right now?

"No problem." He handed her a burger and bag of fries.

"This is an attractive office." She cautiously removed her coat and sat down. "Comfy chair, too." She studied him carefully. "You're sure this is okay, Johnny? I'd hate for you to get in trouble."

"It's fine. Really." He picked up his burger. "Trust me."

After one of the most delicious fast-food meals she could remember, she insisted on cleaning up, trying to leave everything as spotless as they'd found it. Johnny watched with what seemed like amusement. Maybe he wasn't used to anyone cleaning up after him. And then he turned off the lights and locked the door. "Did you bring a list of what you need?"

"To be honest, I probably don't really know what I need."

He chuckled. "Well, let me offer my assistance." He led her over to where painting supplies were stored and started to gather things.

"But can you do this?" she said with concern, "I mean, just borrow these things?"

"Don't forget, you're a Jolly Janitor account."

"Oh . . . right." Still she felt uneasy.

After he'd assembled what seemed a very generous pile of

tools and things, he led her to another section. "Now I'm not sure what you have in mind for a floor, but we just happen to have a bunch of these tiles." He opened some boxes, pulling out some squares of black and white. "I think there's enough to do a checkerboard, but I'm not sure you'd like—"

"I love that," she exclaimed. "That's what Mom originally had in the salon. Have you ever looked at the photos in back?"

He shook his head. "Nope. But you can have these if you want."

"*Have* them?"

"Sure. They're just taking up space and—"

"What is going on here, Johnny?" She pressed her lips together. "I mean, I realize you're a Jolly Janitor employee and Hair and Now is a client. But you can't go around giving their stuff away just like—"

"I can if I want." He reached over to pick up what looked like a can of paint, setting it next to the tile boxes. "You'll need this too, as well as some—"

"Johnny Hollister!" She placed her hands on her hips and glared at him. "I will *not* let you do this."

"Why not?" He grinned. "You won't find a better deal anywhere."

"This is like stealing," she said hotly. "And I'm shocked that you'd even—"

"You really don't know, do you?" He peered curiously at her.

"Know what?"

He waved his hand. "Who owns this business?"

"Huh?"

"I know your mom can't speak. But Ricky didn't tell you? Or Marley?"

"Tell me what?"

"This is *my* company."

"You *own* Jolly Janitors?" Rita almost felt like she needed to sit down. "Really?"

"It was originally my grandpa's business," he explained as he picked up a few other things, setting them down by the boxes of tile. "My dad had no interest in it. He prefers wearing an expensive suit and handling other people's money. But I'd worked for Grandpa, to put myself through college." He went over to get a cart, setting some things on it. "By the time I graduated, Grandpa was getting ready to retire. I had my fancy business degree, so he invited me to step in. After a year or so, he offered to let me take over in exchange for a profit-sharing plan that will see him through his golden years. The business has grown more than either of us expected in these last six years. We're both pretty pleased."

"Wow." Rita slowly shook her head. "And here I was worried that the police were about to show up and drag us both off to jail."

He threw back his head and laughed. "So you really thought I was just an employee? That I was actually stealing this stuff?"

She nodded sheepishly. "It didn't seem like you."

"And you were okay with that?"

She pressed her lips together, not wanting to lie. "To be honest, it bothered me a lot."

"Did it bother you that I was *just* a janitor?"

"I'll admit that I questioned it at first."

He frowned. "You think janitors are second rate?"

"No," she said firmly. "I'm not sure what I thought exactly. Maybe it was that you were too smart to just be cleaning other people's businesses. You know?"

His frown melted some. "Anyway, it's getting late. Let's

get all this stuff to that pallet over there and I'll label that it's taken."

As they quietly worked together, Rita felt silly, and more than just a little embarrassed, for a number of reasons. Worse than that, she felt like a hypocrite and a phony. Discovering that Johnny was not merely a janitor, but the owner of a thriving custodial business, had probably elevated her interest in him. Or maybe it had simply put her more at ease. And even if that was honest, it also seemed wrong. Not to mention shallow. What was wrong with her?

Chapter 10

Johnny had encouraged Rita to take some tile samples to lay out on the floor with the lime green chairs, just to be sure that was what she really wanted. "I don't want to talk you into something just because the price is right," he had joked last night.

On Tuesday morning, she was eager to get to the salon and see if the free tiles really did work. So, before Charlene showed up, she laid out eight squares beside a green chair and decided that it all looked pretty good. Now if only she could get the wall paint right. She'd printed out a number of ideas from the Internet and had narrowed it down to three options, but she just wasn't sure. What she needed was a second opinion. And no one had a better artistic eye than Marley.

"To be honest, I'm not sure about any of these," Marley told Rita as they stood in the salon, where only one customer was getting her hair shampooed by Jillian. Marley pointed out the reasons she questioned each photo then offered another idea. "It seems like a lot of work to rip off that wainscot," she said, "especially when you're so crunched for time. And what if the drywall comes off with it? Then you'd really be in trouble."

"That's true."

"You say you're going to paint those ugly oak cabinets white?"

"To save money."

Marley twisted her mouth to one side. "White is going to show up the wood grain, which is okay if you're going for shabby chic, but that doesn't seem like what you want."

"No, it's not. I'm just trying to save money. I want a somewhat contemporary look—in a retro sort of way."

"Why not paint them black and paint the wainscot to match? Kind of like a wide black stripe going all around. It will really set off those floors and the chairs."

"You don't think that'll be too dark?"

Marley went over to a cabinet, running her hand over the worn surface. "You could top these with something lighter. My brother Gordon's in the quartz countertop business. He might be able to help you."

"Ooh, quartz would be cool."

"And you have to replace those ugly brass drawer pulls." Marley wrote down Gordon's number then pointed at the walls. "And if I were you, I'd paint the walls in a paler tone of the chair color. Kind of a margarita shade."

"Margarita." Rita laughed. "Like my name? Or like the drink?"

"Both."

"Will you help me pick out the color?"

"Absolutely. You gather up some paint samples and I'll

help you decide." Marley pointed up toward the ceiling. "And I'd paint a wide stripe up there—about twelve to eighteen inches I think—in a darker shade of green. Maybe more like the chair color or something in between."

Rita nodded. "I can see that."

"And then I'd paint words right on top of that stripe."

"Words?" Rita frowned.

"Inspiring words," Marley continued. "Something your customers could look up at and feel encouraged by. You know?"

"Maybe..." Rita was trying to imagine the three ladies from the retirement home looking up at words and feeling inspired.

"You can get stencils for letters and signs like that online," Marley explained. "I had one made for my kitchen a couple years ago. An excerpt from the scripture about speaking the truth in love. Rex has probably painted over it by now." She laughed.

Rita made a sympathetic frown.

"This is the name of the company, if you're interested." Marley wrote it down. "Naturally, you'll want to pick a modern style of lettering, something fun that jibes with this whole contemporary thing you've got going on."

"Okay..." Rita looked back at the wall and got an idea. "What about inspiring verbs? Something that suggests action, you know? Like *believe* or *create* or *love* or *embrace*?"

"That would be awesome." Marley nodded. "I can just see it. And if you decide to do that, I'm happy to help with the stenciling. It's actually kind of fun."

"I'll take you up on that."

"You better get right on it then. Make your word list and make sure the company can get the stencils back to you on time. I remember putting a rush order on mine because I was trying to finish up my kitchen in time for book club."

"I'll do it today."

"And get a lot of paint samples for the lime green shades," Marley told her. "Greens can be tricky." Marley went over to a mirror above the cabinet. "What do you plan to do with these mirrors?"

"Well, I'm not a fan of those heavy oak frames, but we obviously need a mirror at each station, and I'd like to avoid the cost of replacing them. I thought maybe I could just paint the frames. Should they be black too?"

"I have an idea." Marley explained how Rita could get small black and white ceramic tiles and make a checkerboard frame that was similar to the floor. "I'll bet you could adhere the tiles directly to these frames since they're pretty flat and fairly wide."

"That sounds perfect." Rita patted Marley on the back. "I knew I called in the right person."

"I'm glad you did. I could do this kind of thing all day. I love design!"

"Well, you've given me fabulous ideas. I owe you big-time."

Marley handed her a list of nearby secondhand stores. "You still have lots of shopping to do. I wish I could join you, but I need to get back to my shop. And don't forget to order those stencils."

After Marley left, Rita got online and found the phone number for the stencil company. A helpful woman promised to get the stencils back within a week if the order was placed by five today. So Rita picked out a contemporary font and, doing the math for how much space each letter took, she started writing down every inspiring verb she could think of, envisioning them circling the salon like a mantra: *believe, nurture, embrace, forgive, give, create, encourage, love, imagine, hope, enjoy, relax, dream, excite, pamper, kiss...* until she had more than enough to fill the walls and, hopefully, a patron's heart. She sent in her order then called Marley's brother Gordon, explaining her need for eight pieces of quartz countertop. "But I'm on a very tight budget," she told him, sharing about how she was doing this for her mom.

"I heard about Donna's stroke," he said. "I hope she's doing better."

"She makes improvement every day. But it's still going to be a long, hard road." She didn't go into the details of Ricky's frustration this morning, or her family's fear that Donna was getting depressed.

"So what sizes are these cabinets?"

She told him the dimensions. "I measured with just a little extra so the quartz would go half an inch bigger than the cabinet top. Does that make sense?"

"Absolutely. And interestingly, I happen to have a lot of remnants in that three-foot range. I hold on to these leftovers in the hopes that someone will need bathroom vanity tops, but they tend to pile up over time."

"Do you have eight white ones?"

"I have tons of white pieces. Do they all have to be the same shade of white?"

She considered this. "I don't see why."

Then he told her his price and she told him she'd take them. "I'll pick out ones that are as similar as I can find. If you're certain about those measurements, I'll go ahead and cut them to length."

"I need to pick them up by early next week, at the latest. Does that work?"

"No problem. And I'll deliver them, Rita. They're pretty heavy."

"Does that cost more?"

"Not for your mom. Did you know that she did Shannon's hair for free when we got married last year?"

"I didn't know that." Rita smiled. "But it doesn't surprise me."

On Wednesday morning, with her notebook and lists in hand, Rita set off to do some serious shopping. Her goal was to hit the discount stores first, to look for the best deals, and to hopefully get everything she'd need before her helpers showed up on Saturday to work. She also picked up a variety of paint samples for Marley to choose from.

"To thank you for your help, I'm buying you lunch, and you're going to let me," she told Marley as they went into Noah's Ark.

"Hey, look over there," Marley nudged Rita with her elbow. "Zinnia and Johnny—under the rainbow."

"Oh . . . ?" Rita just nodded, pretending to be uninterested as she glanced over to where Zinnia was talking animatedly to Johnny.

"Think we should intrude on them like Zinnia did to you the other night?"

"No." Rita looked away. "Of course not."

"I was just kidding." Marley gave Rita a curious look.

"Two wrongs don't make a right," Rita said primly. Okay, she knew she was being silly about this, but something about seeing Zinnia and Johnny just set her teeth on edge. After they received their orders, Rita led the way to the opposite end of the café, as far away from the couple as they could get.

"But your aversion does make me curious." Marley seemed

to be studying Rita closely. "Was there more going on than you let on?"

"What do you mean?"

"I mean, between you and Johnny the other night?"

"I simply offered to buy him dinner to thank him for taking out my trash," Rita said in a way that she knew sounded rehearsed. "No big deal."

"If you say so. I know Zinnia will be relieved to hear that. She was a little concerned."

"Concerned about what?"

"Like I told you, she's had her eye on Johnny for some time now. And with Valentine's Day coming, I think she's actually hoping for a ring."

"*A ring?*" Rita tried not to choke on her tea.

"Okay, that's probably an exaggeration on my part. But Zinnia keeps hinting that he should go shopping at the Jewel Box."

"Seriously?" Rita set down her cup. "Are they even dating?"

"Define dating."

"You know what I mean." Rita glared at Marley.

"Hmm...?" Marley's brows arched. "For someone who claims she's not interested, you seem awfully interested to me."

Rita forced a smile. "I'm just curious, that's all."

"Really?" Marley looked unconvinced.

"You didn't answer my question, Marley. Are Johnny and Zinnia actually dating? Are they a couple? I mean, why would Zinnia say she's hoping for a ring—"

"I take it back, okay? Zinnia merely paused in front of the Jewel Box store window the other day, when we'd gone for coffee. She was drooling over the diamonds, and then she said something about Johnny. I guess I just put two and two to-gether."

"So do you think you're right? Is it really serious between them?"

Marley grinned. "Ooh, so you really *are* interested, aren't you?"

Rita rolled her eyes as she unfolded a napkin. "It's just that you said something that didn't quite make sense to me. I mean, when a woman is hoping for a ring—or simply a piece of jewelry or, well, even flowers—I mean, for Valentine's Day...well, it sounds somewhat serious. Doesn't it?"

"What difference would it make to you?"

Rita grabbed up the oversized bag she was using to haul around all her lists and samples and, eager for a distraction, pulled out her handful of paint swatches. "Help me pick out the wall colors." She splayed them across the table like a green rainbow. "I think this one is nice."

"I can't pick colors out here, silly." Marley swooped up the samples and handed them back.

"Why not?"

"I need to see them with the chair."

"Oh...yeah..." Rita nodded, slipping the samples back into her bag. "That makes sense. That reminds me." She pulled out the fabric swatch she'd gotten from Mr. Cabot last week. "This is for the waiting room chairs. I'm a little wor-ried the print might be too much with the checkerboard floor. But they're already being recovered."

"Sweet." Marley fingered the fabric. "But I agree, it might be a bit much."

"I wondered about a rug beneath the chairs to separate the patterns. Might warm the reception area up a little, too."

"But you'd want a really simple rug. Nothing too busy.

Maybe a sisal or one with solid color blocks of green. Or if you want to be really retro, how about a nice, thick shag? That might be fun."

With Rita's iPad opened to an interior design website, they were busily discussing shag carpet colors when Johnny and Zinnia stopped by to say hello.

Rita tried to act natural as they exchanged greetings. Smiling broadly at Johnny, she tried not reveal how jealous she was feeling—a shade that would go nicely with the paint swatches in her handbag.

"Someone doing some redecorating?" Zinnia nosily peered down at the iPad. "Shag area rugs?"

Rita closed her iPad with the fabric sample inside. Maybe it was juvenile, but she really didn't want Zinnia to know what she was up to. "I thought that might look good in my Beverly Hills condo," she said quickly.

"When do you go back to California?" Zinnia asked with wide eyes. "Frankly, I'm a little surprised you're still here, Rita. Hasn't it been a week or more already?"

"Yes. I'd planned to stay two weeks," Rita coolly explained. "But I decided to extend it to three weeks."

"*Three weeks?* I sure wouldn't want one of my girls to be gone from my salon that long. Hairdressers are so replaceable these days. You must have a very understanding boss."

"You're right. I do." Rita made a stiff smile.

"How's your mother doing?" Johnny asked.

Rita sighed. "She's a little down. They say depression is to be expected with a stroke. But she's always been such a positive, upbeat person—you know, the glass is half full. It's hard seeing her so discouraged."

"Does she still like having visitors now that she's home?" Johnny asked.

"I think she would. But I don't think she's seen anyone but family or her therapists since leaving the hospital."

"I'd like to come see her . . . if you think that's okay."

"Absolutely." Rita nodded. "I'm sure she'd love you to stop by." For that matter, Rita would too—of course, she didn't say this.

"Oh, we should both go see her," Zinnia said eagerly to Johnny. "After all, Donna and I have so much in common—both businesswomen with our own salons. I could chat with Donna about business. Let's do this, Johnny. My schedule's wide open until three thirty."

"Sorry," he told her. "I've got some more appointments and a staff meeting this afternoon."

"Okay, then we'll do it this evening after work," Zinnia said.

"Well, I don't know—"

"Come on, Johnny, let's pay our good friend Donna a visit. We'll take something fun to cheer her up." She looked down at Rita. "Does she like flowers? Candy? Ice cream perhaps?"

"I—uh—I don't know." Rita stared curiously at Johnny. He really didn't seem too thrilled with Zinnia's plan. Would he stand his ground and put the kibosh on this?

"We'll think of something," Zinnia said to Johnny. "Won't we?"

Poor Johnny looked like a deer caught in the headlights. "Is this evening a good time to visit?" he asked Rita in a formal-sounding voice.

"Sure. I can let her know you're coming by."

"Okay then." He nodded, his eyes still locked with Rita's. "Is around seven thirty okay with you?"

"That's fine." Rita would be sure to get home by then.

"Come on, now." Zinnia possessively grabbed his arm.

"We've still got lots to discuss, Johnny Boy." And before any-one could utter another word, Zinnia dragged him away.

"See what I mean?" Marley said after they were gone.

"What?" Rita asked in a somewhat sharp tone.

"Like my grandmother would say, Zinnia has set her cap for him. She's got Johnny Boy on the line, and she is steadily reeling him in."

"Really? What if he doesn't want to be reeled in?"

Marley chuckled and immediately returned to questioning Rita about her sudden interest in Johnny Hollister. "Not that I blame you. Johnny would be a great catch. If my divorce was final, I'd probably go after him myself."

"You would?"

"Sure. Why not? He's a great guy, and I'm sure he'd make a great husband. Not that I have any desire to be married again. Not anytime soon, anyway. But if I was in the market for a good man, Johnny Hollister would definitely rank high on my list."

"Well, if what Zinnia said is true—if Johnny is getting her something for Valentine's Day—you won't have to worry about having him on your list."

Marley laughed. "If I didn't know better—and maybe I do—I'd say that you're feeling jealous of Zinnia right now."

"The only thing I envy about Zinnia right now is her clien-tele list." Rita laid a tip on the table. "I wish I could steal about half of them from her—for my mom."

But as Rita walked back to Hair and Now, she knew that wasn't entirely true. Even if she refused to admit it to any-one—including herself—she was lime green with jealousy.

Chapter 11

Rita called from the salon, warning her family that Johnny and Zinnia were coming to visit this evening.

"Johnny is fine," Ricky said. "But *why* is Zinnia coming?"

"Because she was with Johnny."

"But Zinnia?" He let out a groan. "She's the competition, Rita, the reason Hair and Now hit the skids. Maybe even why Mom had a stroke."

"Oh, that's ridiculous."

"Don't be too sure. Mom was pretty stressed out over the business."

"She can't hear you, can she?"

"No. I'm in the kitchen, cleaning up."

"Look, I'm sorry about Zinnia. Let's just go with it, okay? Maybe it will distract Mom from feeling blue." Then, to cheer her brother up, she filled him in on the latest developments at the salon, making it sound like it was coming along even faster than it really was.

Rita left the salon at seven o'clock sharp, getting home with about ten minutes to spare. She rushed up to her room, the same room she'd inhabited throughout her childhood and was trying not to detest too much now, and hurriedly changed into a pale blue sweater. She freshened her hair and makeup just before the doorbell rang. She hurried back down and was relieved to see that Donna, dressed in lavender velour warm-ups, was seated on the sofa with an expectant half smile. It sounded like her dad was in the family room, watching a basketball game, and Ricky was already answering the door, greeting Johnny warmly and Zinnia stiffly, and taking their coats.

"Mom's in here," Ricky said in a falsely cheerful tone.

"Hi," Rita said nervously as Johnny and Zinnia came into the living room. "Come on in." Everything about this was so awkward, so strange . . . and yet she was glad to see Johnny.

"Hello, Donna," Zinnia said loudly, as if she thought Donna was deaf. "So good to see you. You're looking just fine tonight."

"Hey, Donna." Johnny reached down to grasp Donna's good hand. "You look pretty as always. How are you feeling?"

"Gooo-ood." Donna nodded.

"Brought you some chocolates." Johnny set a red heart-shaped box on the table. "A little early for Valentine's Day, but I couldn't resist."

"Than . . . you . . ." Donna smiled.

"Please, sit down," Rita said to both of them.

"I'll go tell Dad we've got company," Ricky said, backing away. Rita could tell by the spark in his eye that he would not be coming back anytime soon. For that matter, her dad was probably lying low, too.

Johnny sat down next to Donna, looking her directly in her eyes. "Have you been keeping up with your rehab?"

"Yeah."

"And your exercises at home?"

Donna lifted her bad arm with her good one, demonstrating what she'd been working on, trying to move her fingers.

"That's great. You really are making progress."

Zinnia, sitting on the other side of Donna, patted her knee. "I'll bet you can't wait to get back to your salon. I was just telling Rita that I can relate to you. We're both businesswomen, with employees who depend on us." She continued to chatter away as if she and Donna were best friends. To Rita's surprise, her mom seemed to be responding positively. Whether she was simply being polite, or actually enjoying Zinnia's company, it didn't seem to matter. Clearly, Donna was enjoying her visitors.

"Is that the game I hear in there?" Johnny tipped his head toward the family room.

"Yeah." Donna gave him a half smile. "Go...see..."

Johnny patted her shoulder. "A woman after my own heart." He stood, excusing himself. "I'll go pay my respects to Richard and Ricky."

Zinnia looked slightly taken aback by this, and Rita was unsure of what to do. She picked up the chocolates. "Want one, Mom?"

"Yeah..."

"I'll go open them in the kitchen." Rita hurried away, leaving the two businesswomen alone to chat. Okay, she felt a bit guilty, but then wasn't this why Zinnia had insisted on coming, so that she could catch up with Donna?

Rita returned with the opened box, holding it out so Zinnia and Donna could make their selections. "I suppose I should share this with the boys. Right, Mom?"

"Righ...yeah..." Donna waved her good arm. "Go ahea..."

Feeling as if she'd been freed, Rita carried the chocolates into the family room, where the guys were sitting in front of the TV but talking about old cars. Her dad was telling Johnny about the '54 Chevy that he'd been restoring for the past several years.

"I plan to have 'er ready to roll by summer," Richard told him. "There's a big show in Green Bay that I want to take Donna to...I mean, if she's all better by then."

"Mom said to share," Rita said as she passed the big heart around. Then, sitting next to her brother, she pretended to be absorbed with the car conversation and basketball game, but was occasionally sneaking a sideways glance at Johnny.

"Hey, what're you doing in the boys' room?" Ricky poked her in the ribs. "The girls are next door, sis."

"Oh, Zinnia and Mom were having such a good time chatting about their salons. I didn't figure they really needed me."

Ricky rolled his eyes like he wasn't buying that.

"Besides, you know that I like basketball. I played clear through high school, and I'll bet I can still take you." She poked him back.

"Says you."

"There's a hoop in the driveway," Richard reminded them.

"Too bad you're too old to play," Rita teased her dad.

"Says who?"

Suddenly the four of them were out of their chairs and rushing toward the back door like schoolkids. While Ricky dug out the basketball in the garage, giving it a quick pump of air, Richard showed Johnny his car.

"She's a beauty." Johnny ran his hand over the shiny sky blue paint job, pausing to look at her dad's "before" photos of the car. "You've done a beautiful job."

"Thanks." Richard set the photo album away with a proud smile. "It's been good therapy for me. Hopefully I'll have time to get back to it…once Donna gets to feeling better. Maybe this spring."

"You're on my team," Ricky said to Johnny as they exited the garage, out into the cold night air.

"That means you're stuck with me, Dad." Rita took the ball from her brother and dribbled toward the hoop—and suddenly it was game on. But, because of Ricky's bad back, combined with her dad's age, the stiffest competition was between Rita and Johnny. That was fun and loud and lively— and the fouls flowed freely.

Rita was about to shoot what could be the game-winning basket, with Johnny tightly guarding her—so close she could smell his aftershave, a nice woodsy smell—when Zinnia came out, announcing it was time to go. But when Johnny glanced in Zinnia's direction, Rita took her shot, neatly sinking it.

"Nothing but net," Richard said as he gave her a high five. "We win, Princess!"

Johnny pretended to be crushed as he patted Ricky on the back. "Guess we went too easy on the old man and the girl," he joked. "Next time we show them no mercy."

"Nice game," Rita said as she shook Johnny's hand, holding it a fraction longer than necessary as she looked into his eyes. "You're not bad."

"You're not bad yourself." He squeezed her hand with a wink.

As her hand slid out of his, she felt her cheeks growing warm. And it wasn't just from the workout, either.

On Thursday morning, Rita went to the nearby big-box building supply store and, based on Marley's color recommendations, picked out her paint colors. She also found black and white ceramic tiles for the mirrors. But so far she wasn't having any luck with drawer pulls for the station cabinets. She picked up a few other things, and it was past noon by the time she started to make the secondhand store circuit. Her goal was to find some interesting retro items to use as accents. Armed with her paint samples and fabric, she perused the shops and selected some unique pieces. It was time-consuming, but fun. Sort of like a treasure hunt.

By the time she got back to the salon, only Charlene was left, and she seemed to be in a foul mood. When Rita questioned her, Charlene just shook her head. "I'm sorry, but I just think it's useless."

"What's useless?"

"All the trouble you're going to—planning to fix this place up."

"Why is it useless?" Rita set a bucket of paint down by the door.

"It's not going to work."

"Why not?"

"Even if you get it all finished before you leave—which, I'm sorry, but I have my doubts about—it isn't going to feel the same here without Donna." Charlene started to cry. "Donna was the heart of this place, Rita. She's the one who kept us all moving the right direction. I've tried to maintain for her, but I'm not cut out for it. I'm not the leader type." She paused to blow her nose.

"But Mom will come back . . . eventually." Even as Rita said this, she wasn't sure.

"*When?*" Charlene held up her hands. "I popped over to see her during my lunch break. I tried to talk to her and it was so hard. I know she was doing her best, but I couldn't make out more than a word or two. I don't like sounding so negative, but Donna still has a long, long way to go—I mean, before she's ready to come back to work. Even then, she won't be able to cut hair—not with just one hand. And if she can't talk, she won't be much use with customers."

"Stroke patients have been known to recover within six months. Maybe not completely, but she should have her speech back by—"

"Six months?" Charlene blew her nose again. "I didn't want to tell you, Rita, but I'd been thinking about retirement. Donald plans to retire in June, and he'd like to travel some. I want to be free to join him."

"I understand." Rita nodded. "You need to do what you need to do, Charlene. I don't expect you to put your life on hold for the salon."

"But I know you're putting your own savings into this renovation, Rita." Charlene put a hand on her shoulder. "I'm afraid you're wasting your money."

"Well, I think it's a good investment."

"It's a very risky investment." Charlene frowned. "I hope it's an investment you can afford to lose, honey."

"I'm doing it for Mom," Rita said stubbornly.

Charlene reached out to hug her. "You're a good girl, Rita, and I know you want to help your mother. I just hope you won't be sorry . . . that it won't all be for nothing."

Rita hugged her back. "I think we're all under a lot of stress right now. And it's probably going to be even more stressful for the next week or so. In fact, I think you should call it a day now. Go home early. If there are any more appointments, I'll take them."

"There aren't any." Charlene sniffed. "Which is exactly my point. What good is it to fix this place up if we don't have the business to support it in the long run?"

"Don't you worry about that." Rita opened the closet, handing Charlene her coat. "We're going to do everything we can to make this thing work, and if it doesn't—well, they can't say we didn't go down fighting."

But as Rita drove home later that night, Charlene's dismal forebodings were still ringing in her ears. Charlene was right, it *was* a risky investment, and despite her bravado, Rita was getting worried about how much money she was spending. Yet she knew she was being frugal, and that a renovation like she was attempting really should've cost much, much more. She was still mulling these things over when she went into the house.

"How's Mom?" she asked Ricky when she found him in the kitchen.

"She went to bed already," he said glumly. "And Dad's asleep in his chair."

"Oh . . . ?" Rita glanced at the clock. "Kinda early to go to bed."

"Yeah, Mom said she was tired from doing rehab today. But I think she's really just depressed." He scowled. "I know how she feels."

"Oh, Ricky." Rita put a hand on his shoulder. "You're being such a trooper with Mom, but I'm sure it's not easy."

"It's pretty discouraging." He closed the dishwasher so firmly that the dishes inside rattled. "I just keep wondering why our family's been hit so hard these last couple of years.

I mean, first Dad's job gets the ax. Then it's me—getting hurt and losing my football scholarship. Now Mom and this stupid stroke." He frowned at her. "You better watch your back, sis. You might be next."

Rita felt a shiver go down her spine. "Oh, I'm not worried," she assured him, even though she wondered. "And don't forget how our family has had it so good for so many years. I mean, our parents have had a good, happy marriage. We've all had good health...well, until recently. And I know we've never been wealthy, but we've never really gone without, either. Maybe there's good that's going to come out of all this."

"The old 'what doesn't kill you makes you stronger' philosophy?"

She pointed to a dusty plaque that had been hanging by the fridge for as long as Rita could remember. "I know this is what Mom believes, Ricky. I guess I'm trying to believe it too."

Ricky read it out loud. *"We know that for those who love God all things work together for good."*

"It's a good promise." She sighed. "Although a bit open-ended since it doesn't say how long it will take for things to work together for good. I guess that's where faith comes in."

He made a lopsided smile. "I never really thought you were that much like Mom, Rita. But maybe you are. That sounded just like the kind of thing she would've said."

"I wish I was *more* like Mom." Now she confessed to him about how she was more than a little worried about the future of the salon. She even told him about what Charlene had said. "To be honest, I'm feeling pretty overwhelmed. What if Charlene's right? What if we go to all this work for nothing? What if it doesn't work?"

"What do you mean by *doesn't work?*"

"What if we don't increase the clientele? That's what this is really all about. This family needs that business to succeed."

"Oh..." He removed a can of soda from the fridge, loudly popping it. "Is there something more we can do to make sure that it does succeed?"

She got a soda for herself, and as they sat at the kitchen table, she went over her various plans for promoting the salon.

"Those are great ideas." Ricky nodded. "But you know what I'd like to do..."

"What?"

He made what seemed a devious grin. "I'd like to *steal* some business from Zinnia's."

Rita laughed. "Well, so would I. I mean, not *steal*, exactly. But I wouldn't mind if she'd share some with us."

"I'm sure most of her clients used to go to Hair and Now." He held up a finger. "What if I printed out some flyers? Like something we could pass out around the mall? Or maybe stick on cars?"

"People hate it when you hand them stuff or mess with their car."

"What if these flyers had a discount coupon? A lot of people are into saving money with coupons."

Rita considered this. "A coupon...? You know, that's not a bad idea."

"I could make a flyer on my computer and print it out. I could even go to the mall and distribute them for you. I have no problem taking a little flak from folks."

Rita studied her baby brother. Ricky was big and handsome and youthful. "I could imagine some of Zinnia's younger customers eagerly taking a coupon from a guy like you. Especially if you cleaned yourself up a little." She pointed at the front of his torn T-shirt, where something had spilled.

They talked about it some more and finally came up with a solid plan that included a small price increase at the salon. They wouldn't be as expensive as Zinnia's, but they wouldn't be quite so cheap either. "And maybe we can have a members' discount club." Rita paused to make more notes. Eventually they had it all worked out. Ricky would make the flyers with a ten-dollar-off coupon. He'd print them on lime green paper and distribute them during the weekend. Richard would be home and able to give Ricky a much-needed break from helping with Donna.

"This is perfect," Rita said with enthusiasm. "The salon will be closed during the weekend, so no one can go down and see what a mess it is."

"What if they look in the windows?" Ricky asked.

"Oh, yeah. Good point."

"I could cover them with paper for you. With signs saying we're under renovation and when we'll reopen."

"Ooh, I like that. It will make it mysterious."

By the time Rita got ready for bed, she was feeling greatly encouraged. She knew that the hardest work was still ahead, but she felt ready for it. She felt hopeful. As she got into her creaky little twin bed, her thoughts drifted away from the salon and onto something else. Or someone else.

As much as she'd tried not to think about Johnny, it seemed that whenever her guard went down, her thoughts like an arrow went straight to him. She'd replay the times they'd spent together, the conversations they'd had—as well as the numerous times she'd stuck her big foot in her mouth. The bottom line was that she knew she was attracted to him, and sometimes she felt fairly sure he was attracted to her, too.

But what she couldn't wrap her mind around was the Zinnia factor. It just didn't make sense to her that someone like Johnny would be into someone like Zinnia. Not only because Zinnia was a few years older than him, but simply because they were so totally different. Johnny was good and generous and polite and kind. And Zinnia—well, she was just Zinnia. Certainly, Rita was aware that Zinnia was petite and pretty. And she did own a successful business. And sometimes she could actually be surprisingly nice. And it seemed to be true that she'd changed some in recent years, but she was still Zinnia. And as hard as Rita tried to forget some of the less than enjoyable moments with Zinnia, sometimes it was difficult.

Chapter 12

As Rita drove through her parents' neighborhood on Friday morning, she noticed an estate sale sign pointed toward an old but very upscale neighborhood. Although it was bitter cold and windy out, she wondered if it might be worth stopping for, especially since she hadn't had too much luck with the secondhand shops yesterday. She found the house and, seeing it was a well-maintained Victorian, decided to chance it. Several cars and trucks were already parked in front, and people were hurrying inside. Apparently the homeowner had died, and her children were trying to empty the house so that it could be sold.

"The large items are marked," a woman said. "We'll take offers on anything that's not."

Rita hurried through the main area of the house, not seeing anything of interest, but when she reached an upstairs bedroom, she thought she'd won the jackpot. The room was right out of the sixties or seventies. She ran to get one of the cardboard boxes she'd seen by the stairway and quickly began filling it with interesting items. She wasn't sure how much to offer, but hurried down to figure it out and was told the cashier was in the garage. And there, while waiting in a short line, she spotted a couple more treasures. One was a box of colorful Valentine decorations, including several strings of hot-pink heart-shaped lights. The other find was a box filled with old-fashioned clear glass knobs. It wasn't anything like what she'd imagined originally, but the more she thought about it, the more she thought they would work. And from what she could see there would be enough pulls for all the station cabinets. Unless they were terribly expensive, they would be absolutely perfect.

"I'm not sure how to make an offer," she admitted to the gray-haired woman taking money.

The woman frowned at the boxes then shrugged. "Forty bucks for everything seem fair to you?"

"Sure. That sounds more than fair." Rita extracted a pair of twenties from her wallet.

"Well, it's all gotta go. We plan to list the house next week. Tell your friends."

Rita paid her and thanked her, but as she drove away, she felt like a bandit. And as soon as she was in the salon, she texted Marley to tell her about the fabulous estate sale. She unloaded her treasures into the storage room and unlocked the doors. Then, going to the appointment book, she looked over what was scheduled for the few days following the renovation and before the grand reopening. Seeing there were fewer than a dozen appointments, she decided to call every one of them and reschedule them for the following week. She hoped she wasn't being overly cautious, but just in case something took longer than expected, she wanted a little wiggle room. The initial response of some clients was a bit negative, but her offer of a discount for their inconvenience seemed to make up for it.

As usual, Charlene was the first one to arrive, and Rita immediately told her about the promotional plans she and Ricky had made, as well as the ads that would start running by Sunday. "So it's possible we might get people wanting to book appointments while we're renovating," she explained. "I'd appreciate it if you could handle any phone calls while you're here." Charlene agreed to this, but Rita could see the doubtful look in her eyes, as if she thought they were crazy for doing this.

Rita spent the bulk of the day running last-minute errands, gathering supplies, and checking her lists, and by the time she had the salon to herself, she was ready to roll up her sleeves and tear into it. She'd already had the hairdressers empty their stations into boxes that were stored in the back of the storage room, but she decided to empty everything else that wasn't nailed down.

It was past seven by the time she had the place completely stripped. She was just putting some old posters into the extra Dumpster that Johnny had arranged to be delivered to the back door when she saw a familiar red pickup driving past. She waved with enthusiasm, hoping that Johnny would pause to say hi. To her delight, he parked in back and came inside. "I forgot to tell you that no one is cleaning tonight," he said as she closed the door. "Seemed like a waste of effort since we're going to tear into it tomorrow."

"Absolutely." She kicked some pieces of a broken picture frame toward the door. "It's already starting to look like a demo site in here." She led the way to the salon, pointing out to where she'd actually pulled up a piece of vinyl flooring. "I can't wait to see it all torn out."

Johnny reached down and pulled off a piece too. "Looks like this will come up pretty easily. That's good."

She checked him out more closely as he stood. "You look nice, Johnny. Big date tonight?"

He shrugged. "No, not really."

"Well, it *is* Friday." As she wiped her dirty hands on the front of her dirty jeans, she wondered what "not really" meant. Did he actually have a date, but didn't want her to know? "Some people are known to go out on Fridays." She grabbed another corner of the flooring, giving it a firm jerk but only managing to peel off a few inches. She tossed it with the other pieces. "And I'm sure there are plenty of available women who'd jump at a chance to go out with a guy like you." She made a cheesy grin. "Like *Zinnia Williams* for instance." Okay, she instantly regretted the snarky tone in her voice, but it wasn't like she could take it back now.

Johnny looked slightly embarrassed, or maybe just uncomfortable, and she really wished she hadn't said that. She was obviously fishing for information about Johnny and Zinnia. So pathetic. Really, what was wrong with her?

"Sorry," she said quickly. "It's really none of my business who you go out with, Johnny. My bad."

He peered curiously at her. "You really dislike Zinnia, don't you?"

She shoved her hands into her pockets and pressed her lips together, trying to think of an honest answer. "Oh, I don't know that I'd go that far. To be honest I probably don't know Zinnia well enough to dislike her. And I really don't like the idea of disliking anyone. Although I'll admit that I disliked her when she worked for my mom. But to be fair, she was young. So was I. Fortunately, we've both changed." She made a sheepish smile. "Maybe I'm the one who needs to change now, huh?"

"Maybe..."

For some reason that stung. It felt like he was looking right through her and not looking at what he saw. "Look, Johnny," she began slowly. "I think of you as a good friend, okay? And I realize that you might be involved with Zinnia. And although that's absolutely none of my business, it does make me scratch my head. I mean, I don't want to say anything negative, but you seem too good for her." She held up her hands. "There—I've said it. You can say I stuck my big size-eleven foot in my mouth if you want to, but that's the truth. That's how I feel. Nothing against Zinnia."

"Nothing against Zinnia?" He tilted his head to one side like he doubted that.

She shrugged. "Okay, I suppose it sounds like something. Like I'm disparaging her for no good reason. And maybe I am."

"How much do you really know about her?"

"*About* her?" Rita sank into one of the detested pink chairs. "I know that she could be pretty mean—but that was back then."

"Did you know that her parents went through a really nasty divorce when she was eighteen? I think it was right before she went to work for your Mom. I think your mom was kind of like a second mother to her back then."

Rita considered this. "I don't really remember much about Zinnia's family or a divorce." She wanted to add that Marley's parents had divorced about then, too, but it hadn't turned Marley into a bully.

"What did Zinnia do to make you feel so antagonistic toward her?" He sat in the chair across from her.

"Antagonistic?" Rita frowned. Really, was that how he saw her?

"I know there must be some reason, Rita."

"Yeah...there is. But seriously—you want me to tell you about stuff that happened so long ago?"

His brow creased. "Yeah. I'm curious."

Feeling like she was treading on thin ice, Rita began carefully. "Well, Zinnia always had this superior attitude—at least she did toward me. And she had a pretty sharp tongue to go with it. It's ironic, because she's such a petite little thing, I'm sure I could've easily taken her out." She laughed but not with real humor. "Not that I was into that sort of thing. But sometimes Zinnia and I would be the only ones here. Usually, I'd be sweeping up hair, doing laundry, cleaning the back room, folding towels..." She glanced at him. "You know?"

He nodded. "Yeah, I know."

"Without my mom or anyone else around to see her, Zinnia would cut loose and really slice into me—with her mean words."

"Do you think she was jealous?" he asked. "I mean, because of her parents' marital problems, I think she really looked up to your mom. Maybe she was envious of your being Donna's daughter."

Rita considered this. "I guess that could be true. I never really thought of it like that before." And she hadn't—but really, was that an excuse to tear into a person the way Zinnia used to do?

"But I can tell there's more to it," Johnny said softly. "What happened?"

"It seems so juvenile now. I mean, it was so long ago." Rita bit her lip. "But I was still in high school when I helped out here on evenings and weekends. I guess I was pretty insecure." She forced a smile. "You know...being extra tall and stuff. And so when Zinnia would pick on me, like if I was clumsy—and I always felt extra clumsy when she was around. Anyway, it hurt. And then sometimes she'd blame me for things that weren't even my fault. And I wouldn't say anything...I'd just suck it up. And then, even if other people were around, she loved calling me names like Amazon woman and Bigfoot and stupid things like that." Rita felt the old pang of hurt rising up inside of her as she tugged on a loose piece of chair piping, ripping it all the way off. "I know it sounds silly now, but to an insecure and overly tall and gawky teenage girl, it was pretty painful."

He leaned forward with concern in his eyes. "Yeah, I can imagine it was. And I know how Zinnia likes to tease sometimes, but I had no idea she'd ever been such a bully."

"Well, she was barely out of high school herself. And maybe you're right, maybe it had to do with her parents' divorce. Who knows? Anyway, it seems really lame to talk about this now." Rita's face was flushed with emotion and she could feel tears in her eyes, but she was determined not to actually cry. How stupid would that be? "I mean, I realize Zinnia has grown up, Johnny. She's not like that anymore. But sometimes she'll say or do something—maybe even something a little thoughtless—and I probably take it out of context. I react like I'm still an insecure teenager." She made a feeble smile as she stood up. "There, you know how immature I am now." She went over to the sink area to wash the grime from her hands. Suddenly she just wanted to go home.

"I appreciate you opening up like that." He came over behind her. "I can tell that it wasn't easy for you."

"Well, who wants to whine about childish stuff that happened that long ago?" She tore off a paper towel, drying her hands. "And, really, I'm glad that Zinnia's doing so well. And I know I should give her a second chance. Especially since I know she's friends with Marley. And with you, too." She sighed as she tossed the towel in the trash. "In fact, I think it was therapeutic telling you that, Johnny. I don't feel nearly so antagonistic toward her now. Thanks." This time she gave him a sincere smile.

"Glad I could be of help."

She led the way to the back room, turning off the salon lights as she went. "So if you were on your way to take Zinnia out, I hope you both have a wonderful evening. I really do." She got her jacket out of the closet. "I've got to get home now. I didn't realize it was past seven thirty. I missed seeing Mom last night, and I promised not to be too late tonight. I know she's been blue. Dad's bringing home pizza, and we're going to try playing a board game with her afterward. It's a word game her therapist recommended." Rita knew she was babbling as she grabbed her handbag, pulling out her keys. "It's supposed to help her with her speech skills. Hopefully it will work."

"Give Donna my best," Johnny said as she turned out the lights and opened the back door. "By the way, I told Mason and Drew to be here by nine tomorrow. Is that okay?"

"Perfect." She nodded as she locked the door. "Just one more reason I need to hit the hay early tonight. Tomorrow's going to be a big day."

"See you then." Johnny waited for her to get in the car.

She waved then started the engine. She could feel what seemed like a phony smile plastered over her face as she backed out. And then, once she was driving through the parking lot,

she felt the tears coming. She knew it was silly and wasn't even
sure why she was crying like this. Was if from remembering
Zinnia's bullying? Or from the disappointment she'd seen in
Johnny's eyes? Or simply the possibility that those two were
together tonight? Or maybe it was just plain tiredness. Whatever it was, she knew she couldn't help herself.

The next few days passed in an exhausting but productive
blur of tearing out, sanding, patching, taping, removing,
painting, tiling, installing, and cleaning. Everyone was amaz-
ingly helpful, and, thanks to being so busy, Rita and Johnny
never had a chance to talk about anything besides the various
projects. She hoped that awkward exchange they'd had over
Zinnia might be forgotten . . . or at least diminished.

But finally it was Wednesday, and the results of their labors
were truly amazing. Even Rita, who had been seeing it in
her mind's eye for days, was surprised with how perfect it
all looked. From the gleaming checkerboard floors to the
lime green chairs, to the black workstation cabinets with
their clear glass knobs and marble-like quartz countertops,
to the tiled mirror frames against the margarita-toned walls,
clear up to the encouraging words that Rita and Marley had
meticulously applied just below the ceiling line, it was all
wonderful!

"Oh, Rita," Charlene gushed at the end of the day on Wednesday. "You really did it. Everything is absolutely beautiful."

"It's not done yet," Rita reminded her as she arranged the
product that had just arrived from Roberto's on the freshly
painted shelf by the reception desk. "I still have accent pieces
to put up. Marley's going to help with that. And Mr. Cabot
is bringing some of the chairs for the waiting area tomorrow
morning."

"Well, it looks fantastic." Charlene gave a lime green chair a spin. "And everything seems to be in good working order. It's all just fallen beautifully into place."

"So, are you feeling a bit more hopeful now?"

"I am. And I can't believe how many appointments we've booked for the next few weeks. Partly from the ads you've run, but even more seemed to be the result of Ricky's flyers and coupons. That boy really had a good idea with that."

Rita chuckled. "And it doesn't seem to have hurt his love life either. Did I tell you that he inadvertently handed a flyer to a hairdresser from Zinnia's and they've been talking and texting ever since?"

"Oh, dear. Ricky better not get involved with a *Zinnia* girl. No fraternizing with the enemy."

Rita laughed. "Zinnia's is not the enemy. If anything, I should be grateful for Zinnia for leading the way. If I hadn't seen what she'd done with her salon, I might not have been inspired to give this place a makeover."

"So when do we let Donna see it?"

"Not until everything is in place." Rita looked toward the windows, which were still covered with brown kraft paper. "Everyone gets tomorrow off. But I'll come in so Mr. Cabot can deliver the chairs. And I'll do some tweaking and put up decorations for the grand reopening. Let's plan on having Mom here on Friday morning. That way she won't get over-whelmed by too many people, and she can really look around. And the sneak peek for clients doesn't happen until the three in the afternoon. How's that sound?"

Charlene gave Rita another hug. "You are a wonder, Rita. I'm going to hate to see you go next week. You really have to leave on Monday?"

"I do. I promised to be back at work on Tuesday. They're

already getting booked up for the upcoming Oscars." Rita
held up a bottle of shampoo. "And Vivienne was so generous
to give us all this fabulous product. The least I can do is show
up for work on time."

"You will be missed."

Rita sighed, wondering if they would miss her as much
as she would miss them ... and this place. But some things
were better left unsaid. "Hopefully business will pick up
enough that you can hire a new manager soon," she told
Charlene. "Unless you've changed your mind and would consider doing it."

Charlene firmly shook her head no. "I already told you,
Rita, I have no interest in that. I do hair and that's it. You
can't teach this old dog new tricks."

"Well, I'm sure it will all work out. And once Mom sees
what we've done here, I'm thinking it will lift her spirits and
she'll be super-motivated with her rehab. She'll be chomping
at the bit to get back in here. I just know it."

"I think you're right. I can't wait to see her face, Rita. I'm
bringing my camera—I want to capture the whole thing."

That reminded Rita that she still needed to pick up something from the frame shop. She'd had the old photos from
the early days enlarged into black-and-whites, and they were
being matted and framed. She planned to hang them in the
reception area along with a little sign she'd made that said,
THAT WAS THEN ... HAIR IS NOW.

Chapter 13

On Thursday morning, Rita was relieved to have the salon all to herself. The last several days had been such a crazy rush with people working, coming and going, banging and clanging...it was lovely to be able to just quietly putter as she put things away, adding the final finishing touches here and there. Her only interruption was the occasional jangling of the phone—but that was a welcome sound, and she couldn't be happier to book hair appointments. At this rate, they would have to hire more stylists before long. A good problem. However, she was surprised when one call was from Ricky's new friend, Melinda, the hairdresser from Zinnia's. "Ricky told me you might be hiring," Melinda said a bit hesitantly. "I mean, not right now...but sometime in the not too distant future."

"I think that's a real possibility," Rita told her.

"I'd just like you to keep me in mind. I'm still employed at Zinnia's, but I'm not real happy here. But please don't tell anyone I said that. Ricky said I can trust you."

"You can trust me." They talked a bit more, and Melinda even hinted that she had a hairdresser friend who might also be looking for a new job. So Rita wrote down Melinda's number and promised someone would get back to her by early next week. Interesting...

Rita was just peeling the paper from the front windows when she saw Mr. Cabot wheeling the first of the waiting room chairs up to the salon. She held the door as he maneuvered the chair inside.

"It's beautiful!" she exclaimed once they had positioned the green and white chair on the large shag rug that she'd just unrolled.

"White carpet?" Mr. Cabot looked a bit concerned.

"It's made of a fiber that's supposed to be easy to clean." She bent down and brushed her hand over the shaggy loops. "But it's so pretty and luxurious. Don't you love how it looks with this chair?"

He nodded. "Very nice. And now I'll go back for another one."

"How many did you manage to finish?" She asked as she held the door open for his cart.

"All of them." Mr. Cabot grinned.

"You are my hero!" She patted him on the back. "Thank you so much." She followed him outside and stared in wonder at the ice rink. "It's all finished!" she exclaimed. "The ice rink is frozen and ready for skaters."

"Haven't you seen it yet?"

"No." She explained how she'd only used the back entrance these past few days. "And the windows have all been covered with paper." She walked over to get a better look. "It's absolutely beautiful. I'm so glad they brought it back."

"Yes, it will be good for the businesses down here. And

the children will love it." Now he told her about how On Ice had commissioned an ice sculpture for the grand opening on Valentine's Day. "And I heard they're going to drop three hundred red and pink balloons, and they'll have an exhibition with a pair of skaters who were in the last winter Olympics. I don't recall their names. But it will be a very festive day."

"And we'll be having our grand reopening too," she said happily. "It's going to be great."

By one thirty, all five waiting room chairs were in place, and Rita was just hanging the last black-and-white photo when Marley arrived with lunch. "I got tomato and basil soup and sourdough bread," she announced as Rita let her inside.

"Yum!" Rita took one of the bags from her.

"Ooh, it looks beautiful." Marley opened the other bag, removing a large lime green ceramic bowl. "I found this at that estate sale you told me about." She centered it on the glass-topped coffee table in the waiting area then placed three decorative white twine balls inside of it. "How perfect is that?"

"Absolutely perfect." Now Rita led Marley throughout the salon, showing her all the final tweaks and enjoying Marley's reactions.

"I can't believe this is the same salon," Marley said as Rita led her into the back room. "I'm so glad you took before photos. You should put it on Pinterest."

"We'll eat here," Rita set the bag on the lunch table and retrieved a couple of water bottles from the fridge.

"You even redid it back here." Marley sat down at the table.

"It's not as decked out as the salon, but it's definitely better." As they ate lunch, Rita filled Marley in on the upcoming plans. "I hope you can come in for the sneak peek party on Friday."

"I wouldn't miss it."

"I've lined up some yummy appetizers and even bought a case of champagne."

"Ooh, big spender."

Rita chuckled. "It's not an expensive brand. Hopefully no one's a real connoisseur."

"And you still have the grand opening party on Valentine's Day?" Marley asked.

"Yes. The grand reopening is Sunday." Rita sighed. "And then I fly out Monday morning."

"I bet you're looking forward to that warm California sunshine."

Rita nodded. "It's been pretty chilly here."

"I hear we're supposed to get snow this weekend." Marley shook her head. "I'm ready for spring to come."

"You should come visit me in California."

Marley's eyes lit up. "Yeah, I'd love to. I've never been there before."

As they finished up, Rita pulled out a calendar and they talked dates that might work for Marley to make the trip. "As long as I can find someone reliable enough to manage the shop for a few days. Maybe my mom could do it." Marley tossed her emptied soup container in the trash. "Speaking of the shop, I better get back."

"Thanks for lunch."

"Oh, yeah, I almost forgot." Marley made a slightly sheepish face. "Zinnia wants to come down here and see the salon."

"Oh...?"

"Sounded like she was going to pay you a visit today."

Rita grimaced. "Oh...okay."

"I think she's worried."

Rita laughed. "Well, that's ridiculous."

"Anyway, just wanted to let you know."

"Thanks." Rita wasn't overly eager for Zinnia's visit, but she did appreciate the heads-up. No doubt Zinnia wanted to check out the competition—and hadn't Rita done the same a couple weeks ago? As she cleaned up the lunch things she noticed how quiet the salon was and remembered the CDs she'd picked up for her mom's old CD player the other day. She knew her mom loved listening to an oldies radio station—both at home and at the salon—but Rita wasn't a big fan of the multitude of weird ads that were played between songs. For that reason, she'd gotten a package of golden oldies CDs. Enough for hours of "easy listening." Maybe someday she'd talk Donna into an MP3 player, but for now it was better than radio ads.

With songs from the sixties and seventies playing, Rita got out the Valentine's decorations she'd found at the estate sale and went to work filling the front windows. She had just plugged in the strings of hot-pink heart-shaped lights, which looked absolutely perfect, when she spied Zinnia striding up to the salon like she was on a mission.

"We're not open," Rita told her after she unlocked and opened the door.

"That's okay. I'm not here to get my hair done." Zinnia laughed like this was funny.

"No, I didn't think so." Rita stepped back. "Want to come in?"

"Thank you." Zinnia walked in with an air that seemed to suggest superiority, but maybe Rita was just being judgmental again.

Remembering what Johnny had said last week, Rita was determined to be more gracious. To break the ice, she explained about how the chairs had been recycled. "Everything had to be done on a shoestring budget," she told Zinnia. "But it was fun. And I think my mom will be pleased."

"Well, it's quite a transformation." Zinnia frowned. "But that's not why I'm here. I have a bone to pick with you, Rita. Several in fact."

"Really?" Rita folded her arms across her front. "What's that?"

"I don't like that your brother's been sniffing around my salon, attempting to steal my patrons and flirting with my employees and—"

"*What?*" Rita felt immediately defensive of her baby brother.

"That's right. I saw him out there handing out flyers. And I know that he's been talking to Melinda."

"Ricky and Melinda are both interested in each other, Zinnia. Surely, you can't tell your employees who they can or cannot date."

"And what about stealing my customers? Not to mention my employees?"

"What are you talking about?"

"I overheard a couple of my girls talking, Rita. I know that you're trying to lure them away."

"We're not trying to lure anyone away. We simply want this salon to thrive like it used to thrive."

Zinnia narrowed her eyes. "I know what you're up to, Rita."

"What am I up to?" Rita calmly asked her.

"You're trying to get back at me. To get even."

"Get even?" Rita studied her closely, watching as Zinnia nervously picked at her cuff. "For what?"

"You *know* what." Zinnia put her hands on her hips and stuck her chin out.

"Are you talking about how you used to treat me?" Rita tipped her head to one side, waiting. "Back when I was still in high school and you worked for my mom?"

"Johnny told me all about it."

Rita took in a sharp breath. *Really?* Was it possible that Johnny had betrayed her confidence like that? *How dare he!*

"Don't act so surprised, Rita. What did you expect him to do? Johnny and I are very close. Why wouldn't he tell me?"

Rita slowly shook her head, trying to sort out all the crazy conflicting feelings that were raging through her. "Zinnia," she said evenly. "Why exactly are you here?" There was a long pause and Rita silently counted to ten, willing herself to remain calm.

"Look, I know I was horrible back then," Zinnia said unexpectedly. "I can admit that much. But I was young and dumb...and besides, that was a long time ago. Can you really hold that against me all these years later? What about letting bygones be bygones?"

Rita shrugged. "Hey, I'm happy to forget about all of that."

"Good." Zinnia nodded with a slightly triumphant twinkle in her eyes. "And I'm sorry I was such a witch back then. But I *have* changed, Rita. I really have. You need to give me a second chance."

"I've been trying to do that."

"And I know you'll be gone soon...back to sunny Beverly Hills and all your celebrity clients. Lucky girl."

"Right..." Rita felt slightly off balance, like something about this conversation wasn't quite on the up and up.

"All right then." Zinnia looked around the salon again. "So you're really not trying to get even with me?"

"I'm not trying to steal anyone's employees or customers,

Zinnia. But it's a free country. Surely you recognize that people will come and go."

"I suppose. But that's not the only thing I thought you were trying to steal."

"*Really?*"

"Oh, Rita, I'm not blind. I know that you've been after Johnny ever since you got back here. Even Marley suspects you've been crushing on him."

Rita felt betrayed again—this time by Marley. She also felt confused and couldn't help but remember how mean and manipulative Zinnia used to be. Was it possible she was doing it again? Somehow Rita had to get to the bottom of this. If that was even possible.

"Johnny has been a good friend to me," Rita said in voice much calmer than she felt. "I never could've finished this renovation without his generous help. I'm grateful to him. But that's where it ends."

"Johnny helped you redo this place?" Zinnia looked seriously aggravated, and for some reason that was satisfying. Childishly satisfying.

"I'm surprised he didn't tell you." Rita studied Zinnia as she spoke. "Didn't you wonder why Johnny had been so unavailable this past weekend?"

"We were both busy..." Zinnia glanced away.

Now Rita was getting even more suspicious. "Just how close are you two anyway?"

"I don't think that's any of your business."

"Except that Johnny is my friend."

"He's my friend, too!"

"I know. Johnny has made it clear to me that he *is* your friend, Zinnia. And Johnny is a very loyal friend. He's Marley's friend, too. And he's even my mom's friend. Come to think of it, Johnny has quite a number of friends." It was like a lightbulb was going on inside her head. "Is it possible that you and Johnny are only *just* friends, Zinnia, but perhaps you're trying to make it into something bigger?"

Zinnia's features tightened—as if Rita had hit a nerve.

"Marley gave me the impression that you have some pretty high expectations of your relationship with Johnny," Rita persisted. "Is that true?"

Zinnia shrugged, sauntering toward the door as if she was finished with her confrontational visit.

"Or did you say those things to Marley simply because you knew she would tell me, and you knew that would make me back off... kind of like protecting your property?" Rita got in front of Zinnia, making it to the door first.

"That's perfectly ridiculous." Zinnia glared at her.

"What was your real reason for coming down here, Zinnia?" Rita kept her hand on the door, blocking Zinnia from exiting. "Did you think you could intimidate me? About this salon? About my brother? About future customers and employees? About Johnny? Because that's what it feels like to me." She sighed. "I'm happy to let bygones be bygones and to forgive and forget, but I don't think that's what you really had in mind. Did you?"

With narrowed eyes, Zinnia shook her finger in front of Rita's face. "You should talk. Despite what you say, I know you're doing all this to get back at me. You never liked me. You always thought you were better than me just because your mom owned this shop. Admit it!"

"That's ridiculous. I've never—"

"You came back here thinking you could ruin my life, Rita. But you'll see that it's not that easy—"

"If anyone's going to ruin your life, Zinnia, it will probably be you." Rita opened the door. "Thanks for stopping in." As Rita locked the door, she couldn't help but feel she'd just been hijacked onto an emotional roller-coaster ride. But she also felt like she'd finally stumbled onto the truth. Johnny had been partly right about Zinnia being jealous of Rita way back then. But, perhaps more importantly, Johnny was no more involved with Zinnia than he was with Marley or her mother or even Rita herself, for that matter. Johnny was simply being Johnny—a good guy and a loyal friend. He had too much sense to get pulled in by someone like Zinnia. And, as she turned off the salon lights, Rita actually felt a small wave of pity for Zinnia. Maybe she'd changed a little since those old days, but she still had a ways to go.

Chapter 14

Rita insisted on helping with her mother's hair and makeup on Friday morning. "I know you've been practicing doing it yourself," Rita said as she ran the smoothing iron over the last strand of her mom's platinum hair, "but it's okay to be pampered sometimes. You deserve it."

Donna muttered a fairly intelligible thank you. "Your speech is really improving," Rita told her. "But I hope you won't feel the need to converse with everyone today. I'm sure it'll be overwhelming. Just try to enjoy. We all understand that you've been through a lot these past three weeks. The girls are just excited to see you." She straightened the collar of Donna's pale pink blouse. "You look so pretty, Mom. No one would guess that you'd recently suffered a stroke."

Donna pointed to her limp right hand and sadly shook her head. "This...arm. Not good."

Rita knew her mom was uneasy about being in public

again. And she just wanted her to relax and feel at ease. "People only notice your arm if you point it out." Rita picked up the fluffy blush brush, giving her mom's cheeks one last swoosh of color. "Even your face is pretty much back to normal. Have you noticed how much it's improved? Unless you smile really big, it's hard to see any paralysis."

"It's better." Donna gave her a small smile. "See..."

As Ricky drove them to the mall, Rita tried to play down the improvements they'd done at the salon. "As you know our budget was pretty limited," she told her mother. "But we did our best. I just hope you like it." As Ricky drove through the mall parking lot, Rita warned her mom that they were going to blindfold her. "I don't want you to see it until you're all the way in there."

At the back door, Rita pulled out a silk scarf. "Close your eyes, Mom." Donna giggled as Rita loosely tied the scarf around her head. "No peeking."

"I haven't seen it either," Ricky admitted as the three of them went inside. "Not since I finished painting, anyway."

"We're just going through the back room now," Rita explained. "And here we are in the salon." She grinned at Charlene and Jillian and Yolanda. "The gang's all here." After Charlene nodded that her camera was ready, Rita untied the scarf and watched as her mother's face lit up.

"Oh—my—oh—my!" Donna started to cry. But Rita knew they were happy tears. Donna continued to exclaim "oh my!" as she went around the salon, touching the chairs and examining everything. She was more than just pleased, she was ecstatic. And Rita could not have been happier.

"You really like it?" Rita finally said.

"Love...it." Donna tightly hugged Rita with her one good arm. "Thank you, Rita."

"I have something else to show you. In fact, I want you all to see this." Rita led them up to the reception desk, where she opened the appointment book. "Eventually you will be able to enter appointment bookings just on the computer," she explained. "But for now we can do both." She opened the book and showed them how many appointments had been booked for the next several weeks. She pointed to Saturday. "As you can see we have a busy day tomorrow. Lots of new customers, too. So everyone will get a full eight hours."

Donna pointed to the column where Rita had inserted her own name. "You are working, too?"

Rita grinned. "That's right. We were so busy that I decided to take appointments, too. Hair and Now is getting back on its feet, starting tomorrow."

Donna's eyes filled with tears again. "Oh...my..." She shook her head in wonder. "This is good. So...good."

As Rita closed the book, she noticed a delivery man at the door. Although the salon wasn't officially open, she unlocked the door and was pleasantly surprised to see that he had an enormous bouquet of bright red tulips.

"Whooo?" Donna asked Rita, sounding a bit like an owl.

Rita peeked at the card. "Congratulations to Hair and Now on your grand reopening, from Jolly Janitors," she read.

Donna slowly nodded. "J-John."

As Rita placed the pretty arrangement on the reception desk, she told herself that this gift was simply from a business to a business—but she wished it was something more. Although she knew she didn't deserve it.

Everyone snacked and visited for more than an hour, and Donna was holding up pretty well, making some really good attempts at conversation. But as it got closer to the time for the sneak peek party to begin, Rita grew concerned. "I invited all of your old clientele, Mom. And I'm sure they'd love to see you, but I don't want to wear you out."

"I don't know..." Already Donna had declared she wouldn't stay for the rest of the festivities, but she'd been having such a good time that Rita wanted to make sure.

"We'd love to have you stay, Mom, but if you're tired, we understand."

Donna looked slightly torn, but finally turned to Ricky. "Home..." she told him. "We'll go home...that's good."

Everyone hugged and said goodbye and Rita reminded Donna that it wouldn't be long before she'd be spending whole days here again. "You just need to get stronger, Mom." She kissed her cheek. "Keep working at your exercises."

Donna linked her arm in Ricky's. "Yeah. I will. Ricky will help."

The rest of the afternoon was spent meeting and greeting old customers, many who hadn't been into the salon for years, giving them personalized tours, making them feel welcome, replacing appetizers and refilling glasses, and booking yet more appointments. By the time the last of the guests left at around six, Rita felt socially exhausted, but happy.

She took her time cleaning up the remains of the party and putting the salon back into working order. It wasn't until she was taking a trash bag out to the Dumpster that she realized she was stranded. Because Ricky had driven them here and then taken Donna home, she was without wheels. Not only that, but she knew that Ricky was taking Melinda out tonight. She considered calling her dad to pick her up, but knew he'd be home by now, probably with his feet up.

As she went back inside, she called Marley, explaining her situation.

"No problem," Marley assured here, "but I have to stay here until closing. I'm by myself, too, or I'd offer to run you home."

"That's okay. I'll just stick around until nine." Rita peered out the front entrance as she unplugged the Valentine lights.

"That's two hours," Marley pointed out. "What'll you do?"

Rita looked out at the ice rink, where, to her surprise, several people were already skating. "I think I just found something to occupy me." She giggled. "I will be putting myself On Ice."

"What?"

"Skating. I'm going ice skating!"

Marley laughed.

"So, I'll see you around nine." Rita eagerly grabbed her coat.

"Be careful," Marley said. "And don't break anything."

It wasn't until Rita reached the On Ice entrance that she noticed the "closed" sign. Standing by the gate, she felt like the hungry kid with her nose pressed against the candy-shop window. "Are you really closed?" she asked a gray-haired man who was walking through the darkened lobby area. "I saw skaters out there and thought..."

"We're not officially open," he explained.

"Oh... sorry to bother you."

"It's just our On Ice employees and some mall employees, sort of testing it out."

So she explained about Hair and Now's reopening. "And it's so fun to coincide with On Ice. I love that the ice rink is back. I used to skate here all the time as a kid."

"You a pretty good skater?" He grinned as he unlocked the gate.

"I was okay." She felt a surge of hope.

"Come on." He jerked his thumb toward the rows of skates behind him. "What size you need?"

"Elevens." She laughed. "Yeah, I know. *Bigfoot.*"

He smiled as he set the skates in front of her. "I'd never call such a beautiful young woman Bigfoot. Have fun, kid."

She did feel like a kid as she sat down to lace up her skates. She extracted her leather gloves and the silk scarf she'd used to blindfold her mom, before she deposited her handbag and boots in a locker. Tying the scarf around her chin, she realized her corduroy skirt and tights weren't the best outfit for skating, but if she moved fast enough, she'd probably stay warm.

At first she felt a little unsteady on the slippery ice, but before long she was moving along fairly gracefully. She could feel the wide smile on her face as she swayed from side to side, gliding happily around the gleaming ice. This was wonderful, amazing—the next best thing to flying. The other skaters all seemed to be enjoying themselves as much as she was. It was like a small private party. To her delight, she still knew how to skate backward, and after awhile, she even attempted a spin and was relieved to remain upright. Skating, it seemed, was like riding a bike... one didn't forget.

After about an hour of vigorous skating, she felt herself wearing out. She slowed down, deciding it was a good time to take a break. She was about to exit the rink when she heard someone coming from behind—and moving fast. Unsure of which side the skater would pass on and worried they might collide, she glanced over her shoulder and was shocked to see it was Johnny! In that same instant, her skates slipped and she felt herself falling backward—straight into Johnny's path. It was going to be ugly.

Hoping she wasn't about to wipe out Johnny, she braced herself for pain. But instead of slamming onto the rock-hard ice, she felt a strong arm swoop around her, and, as Johnny pulled her snugly next to him, she remained on her skates.

"Sorry to startle you like that." With his arm still wrapped around her waist, he guided her to the side rail, where she stared at him in wonder.

"I can't believe you actually kept me from falling." She laughed nervously. "I thought I was a goner for sure—and probably taking you down with me."

He smiled. "I thought you made a rather graceful recovery."

"Only because you saved my bacon." She made a relieved sigh. "Thanks."

"I only saved you after I spooked you. Stupid move on my part." He reached over to push a strand of hair away from her face. "Sorry."

"I was getting tired," she admitted. "I'd been going at it pretty good for an hour. I was probably an accident just waiting to happen."

"Can I join you in a break?" he asked with hopeful eyes.

"Sure." She nodded eagerly.

"I'm guessing you haven't had dinner yet." He rested his hand on her back as they exited the rink.

"As a matter of fact, I haven't," she confessed. "Other than a few appetizers, I haven't had lunch, either."

"It's late enough, we might be able to get a table at Noah's Ark."

Before long, they had turned in their skates and were on their way up the escalator. "How did you get the old guy to let you in?" she asked Johnny.

"On Ice is one of my accounts. I'd been invited."

As they strolled down the mall, he asked about her day and she told him all about her mom's wonderful reaction as well as the sneak peek party. "And we've got a full day of appointments booked for tomorrow. And lots more for the rest of the month."

They were soon seated at a table in Noah's Ark. Once again, there were candles and tablecloths, and it didn't quite seem like the same café. But Rita was so happy to be here with Johnny that she wanted to pinch herself.

"What a happy coincidence," she declared, "meeting you like that at the ice rink. Especially since it wasn't officially opened."

"I have to confess that it wasn't completely serendipitous. I knew you were down there," he said. "I spoke to Marley a little while ago."

"Oh...?"

"So bumping into you wasn't a true coincidence." He chuckled. "Well, not that I meant to *bump* into you. Not like that anyway."

"Well, I was hoping I'd get to talk to you before I went back to California," she admitted after their orders were taken.

"When do you leave?"

"My flight's Monday morning—early. And tomorrow I'll be doing hair all day. And then Sunday's the big grand reopening celebration. So I'm glad I ran into you tonight."

He smiled. "Me, too."

As much as Rita longed to keep their conversation light and bright and upbeat, she was distracted by something. Finally, she just blurted it out. "Zinnia paid me an unexpected visit."

His brows lifted. "She did?"

"Yes...and she was rather forthcoming..." Rita arranged her words carefully. "I mean, about her relationship...with you."

"Forthcoming? About me? What do you mean?"

"Well, she's obviously very into you, Johnny." She made a half smile. "Can't blame her for that. But I was a little disturbed when she informed me that you'd repeated something I'd said to you the other night. Something I thought I'd said in confidence."

He frowned. "I only told Zinnia that I thought you ladies had some old unresolved issues. I didn't go into any detail whatsoever, Rita. Mostly I was just trying to get Zinnia to own up to her part of the problem. The truth is she seemed slightly obsessed with the idea that you were trying to ruin her business." He made a rueful smile.

"I thought it might've been something like that," Rita confessed in relief. "But I just wanted to hear it from you."

"That's how it happened. I guess I shouldn't be surprised that Zinnia might twist it around. Her perceptions aren't necessarily reality."

Rita just nodded.

"I try to remain on congenial terms with all my cleaning accounts," he continued. "I want to treat them like friends. But sometimes it gets complicated."

"You mean like when the women get overly interested in you?"

He shrugged. "There's a fine line. And I told Zinnia that she had crossed it."

"Oh..."

Suddenly the conversation ceased, and they both just sat there looking across the table at each other, saying nothing, just gazing into each others' eyes. It was a long, slightly breathless sort of moment, and Rita got the impression Johnny was about to say something important. But that was just when Rita noticed a pair of familiar women entering the café.

"Don't look now." She tipped her head toward the en-trance. "But Zinnia and Marley are here. Looks like they're headed our way. Déjà vu." She chuckled.

"Let's not invite them for dessert this time."

"Deal," she whispered.

"Hello, kiddos." Zinnia's tone seemed borderline snotty. "How was the ice rink?"

"Nice," Johnny said lightly.

"I'll bet." Zinnia glared down at Rita.

"Did you even remember how to skate?" Marley asked with a grin, apparently unaware of the awkward dynamics devel-oping here.

"Pretty much," Rita said. "I was just quitting when I bumped into Johnny."

"*Literally*," Johnny added, making Rita giggle.

"Do you still need a ride, Rita?" Marley asked.

"I can take her home," Johnny said quietly.

"I'll bet you can," Zinnia retorted.

Hoping to lessen the tension, Rita explained about being without a car. "I didn't even figure it out until closing time."

"It's not out of my way to drop you off," Marley assured her.

"Thanks." Rita gave Marley a stiff smile, wishing she could tip her helpful friend off, and let her know that she was happy to ride with Johnny. "But we might not be finished eating by the—"

"No problem," Marley said obliviously. "We haven't even ordered yet."

"Come on." Zinnia glowered at both of them as she grabbed Marley by the arm. "Let's get our table."

"Wow," Johnny said quietly. "If looks could kill."

"The coroner would be on his way."

"I have a feeling I'm about to lose my Zinnia's account."
Johnny chuckled as if this was of little concern, but Rita was
not so sure. Zinnia was not the kind of person you wanted for
an enemy. Of course, once Rita was out of the picture, Zinnia
might cool off. Eventually.

"I'm so sorry," Marley said for the umpteenth time. "I feel
like such an imbecile. I honestly had no idea what was going
down tonight, Rita. I thought you and Johnny were just
friends. I really did."

"I know. I was trying to make myself think the same
thing," Rita admitted. "And, honestly, it would've been easier
on everyone—especially Zinnia—if I still believed that."

"But you don't, right?"

"I can't deny there's a strong attraction..."

"And you think it's mutual?"

"I don't know... maybe... not that it matters."

"Because you're leaving on Monday?"

Rita nodded sadly. "I've got to get back to my life. I've
stayed so long that my job could be at stake."

"But what about Johnny?" Marley sighed in a romantic
sort of way. "He's obviously into you. I should've figured that
out when he came by my shop to ask about your whereabouts
tonight. But I assumed it was something in regard to cleaning, you know, for the grand reopening party. Plus I was
distracted with a customer at the time."

"At least you told him where to find me."

"I guess. But then I stupidly walk up to your table—with
Zinnia." Marley groaned. "How lame was that?"

"You didn't know what was going on."

"Well, I knew how Zinnia felt about Johnny. And I
should've known, based on the snarky things she's been say-

ing about you lately, that she's extremely jealous. Seriously, I thought she had changed. But I'm starting to wonder. You should've heard her after we sat down at our table. I had no idea she still had that kind of mouth on her."

Marley pulled into the driveway at Rita's parents' house. "Well, at least Johnny gets it now," Rita said. "He's seen some of Zinnia's true colors."

"And she's got plenty."

"I feel relieved to know he's not interested in her." Rita reached for her handbag. "Talk about a bad match."

"I really am sorry that I didn't—"

"It's okay, Marley." She patted Marley's shoulder. "It's probably for the best. I mean, it's not like Johnny and I could've figured this whole thing out during the short drive over here. Not that there's anything to figure out. Besides that, I'm pretty worn out from today."

"If I don't see you tomorrow, I'll see you on Sunday," Marley called as Rita got out. "At your reopening party."

Rita waved. "Thanks for the ride." As she went into the house, she replayed the moment on the ice—when Johnny had come up from behind, when he had caught her. She was well aware that she was not petite. Nothing like Zinnia... And she knew it took a big, strong guy to keep her from falling like that. A guy like Johnny.

Chapter 15

Saturday passed in a happy blur of activity. It was wonderful to see the salon bustling with activity, with all four hairdressers busily attending to clients. "You're going to have to hire more help," Rita told Charlene as the two of them took a quick break in the back room. "Melinda, for starters. And then maybe her friend, too."

"Zinnia will throw a fit."

"Maybe...unless her business slows down enough that she doesn't need so many hairdressers."

"And you think she won't throw a fit about that?"

Rita considered this. "You're probably right." Suddenly she remembered something her last appointment had inquired about. "But there might be a way we could attempt to smooth things out with her."

"Really?" Charlene looked skeptical.

"We are strictly a hair salon," Rita pointed out. "That's the way Mom wants it. But some of our clients are interested in manicures and other services. What if we worked out a deal with Zinnia? We could promise to send them her way . . . maybe even keep some of her business cards here . . . or schedule our clients' hair appointments to mesh with appointments at Zinnia's."

"In exchange for what?"

Rita shrugged. "Goodwill?"

Charlene laughed as she set her coffee mug in the sink. "I suppose it would be worth a try."

"I think Mom would like it," Rita said as she tossed her empty water bottle in the trash. "She actually likes Zinnia."

Charlene wrinkled her nose. "There's no one your sweet mother does not like."

"I guess we could all take lessons from her."

For the remainder of the day, while Rita was washing, cutting, and styling hair, she toyed with the idea of trying to get along with the salon upstairs. And she realized that once she was out of the picture and her mom came back to work, it might actually be doable.

By quitting time, Rita was exhausted. She was thankful that tomorrow's grand reopening wouldn't involve any hair appointments. As she went outside to the car, she remembered the couple of times that Johnny had parked his big red pickup back here. She peered up and down the lane, but there was no sign of it or him. And she was too tired to be concerned.

On Sunday morning, Rita slept in. The reopening party wasn't scheduled until one, and she decided to use this luxurious leisure time to catch up with some of her own beauty treatments. She knew that her mom didn't care to attend today's party, and she didn't blame her for that. If Rita could've opted out of the festivities, she would've gladly done so. Especially knowing that she'd have a long flight tomorrow—and then it would be back to the old grindstone on Tuesday. What a way to use her vacation leave.

"Happy Valentine's Day," Richard called out when she came into the kitchen. "I got some of my heart-shaped flap-jacks left here, if you're interested."

Still in her bathrobe and an old pair of her mom's fuzzy slippers, she came over to admire her dad's culinary skills. "I almost forgot about these." She picked up a lopsided golden heart and took a nibble. "Yum. Count me in."

"Your mom and Ricky already ate." Her dad filled a plate for her. "But I wanted to make sure there were some left for you." He set it in front of her. "Coffee?"

"Please." She gave him an appreciative smile.

"I want you to know how much it means to your mom and me, what you did for the salon, Rita." He set a chipped mug on the table. Decorated with a big pink heart that said I LOVE YOU, she remembered how she'd painted it at a ceramics shop back when she was about ten—then given it to her mom on Valentine's Day.

"I can't wait for you to see it."

"Ricky showed me some photos on his phone last night. It looks great." He leaned down and kissed her on the cheek. "I'm so proud of you, sweetie."

"You need to come by and see it," she told him. "Maybe you could swing by the reopening party today."

"I suggested that to your mom, promising that we wouldn't stay long, and she sounded up for it."

"Great!"

Richard sat down across from her with his coffee. "I can't believe you're leaving tomorrow, Rita. It seems like you just got here. You've been so busy with the salon. And I've been so busy with work and helping your mom. Well, it just went by too fast."

"I know. But maybe it'll motivate you to bring Mom out to California." She held up her coffee mug like a toast. "And with as much business as Hair and Now is going to get, here's to you being able to afford it, too."

He clicked his mug against hers. "Here's to it."

She filled him in on some of the recent developments at the salon, saying how it would be necessary to hire more hairdressers soon. "I think we could have all eight stations running by summer."

"And hopefully your mom will be ready to go back by then...or soon."

"She seems to be recovering...if she sticks with her rehab."

"Well, you've given her motivation, Rita." Her dad sighed. "Thank you."

The reopening party, thanks to Ricky handing out more flyers to people who were attending the opening of On Ice, was even busier than Rita had expected. And when her parents popped in, just an hour before it was supposed to end, it was fairly crowded. "I think it's a success," she whispered in Donna's ear.

"Thanks to you," her mom mumbled back.

Rita hugged her. "Thanks to you, too," she said. "Remember this was originally *your* dream."

Donna smiled with teary eyes. "Our dream."

Finally, the food and champagne were gone and the last guests had just exited, so Rita took this opportunity to lock the door. She was just starting to clean up when she heard someone in the back room. Thinking it was someone who'd been locked in, she hurried to see. "Johnny!" she exclaimed.

"Sorry to startle you." He removed the trash bag from her hand. "But this isn't your job, Rita."

"I know. But it's Sunday and I know we're not scheduled for cleaning—"

"You are tonight." He smiled. "You look very pretty."

She glanced down at the magenta dress she'd worn for the party. "I was trying to be festive."

"Perfect for Valentine's Day. But I'm not sure about skating."

"Skating?"

"Don't you want to? I mean, especially after I cut your time short the other night."

"Sure," she said eagerly. She looked back down at her dress, thankful she'd chosen this one, with its fuller longer skirt, instead of the short fitted red number she'd almost worn. "And I think this will be just fine for skating."

"Will you be warm enough?"

"As long as I keep moving."

Before long, they were out on the ice—along with about a hundred other people. But it was fun and, thanks to her practice the other night, she felt like she was in top form. "You're a good skater," she told Johnny as they skated side by side with arms linked together.

"So are you," he said. "And thanks to your lovely long legs our strides seem to match."

She nodded, feeling the warmth rising in her cheeks. "Oh, look at that!" She pointed to a heart-shaped ice sculpture that was illuminated with lights that made it look pink. "It's so beautiful." And suddenly she remembered the dream she'd had—three weeks ago—and it felt almost as if she were reliving it now. "So amazing."

Johnny nodded. "And romantic."

"Yes...it is." She got another warm rush, followed by a slightly dizzy and lightheaded feeling. "It's exquisite," she murmured, tightening her hold on his arm and hoping she wasn't about to faint.

They made several more laps around the rink and then Johnny pointed upward to the skylights three stories above. "Look, it's starting to snow."

She stared up in wonder. "I'd been wanting it to snow!" she exclaimed. "Ever since I got here. It's been so cold...but no snow."

"Well, it's coming down now." He guided her to the edge of the rink so they could watch it falling.

"So beautiful." She shook her head. "It makes me sad."

"Sad?" Johnny frowned.

"Because I have to leave tomorrow."

"Oh..." He nodded sadly.

She gazed across the magical rink, marveling at how lovely the ice looked, illuminated by the pastel tinted lights. "It's all so perfect...so beautiful—" She let out a little gasp. "It's just like I dreamed!"

"You dreamed about this?"

She took in a steadying breath as she studied the ice. "Well, not exactly. But I did have an ice-skating dream... while I was still in California."

"*Look!*" Johnny pointed upward again.

"The balloons are falling!" She watched as pink and red balloons tumbled down from the top floor of the mall. Skaters laughed and dodged the balloons as they bounced on the ice. Children squealed with delight trying to capture them. And soon the ice rink turned into a lively pool of pink and red balloons.

"Happy Valentine's Day!" Johnny said brightly.

"Happy Valentine's Day to you, too." She knew her words sounded flat compared to his.

"What's wrong?" he asked with concern.

"It's just that ... well, I feel like—like I've come home."

"Maybe you have."

"But I have to go tomorrow."

"Why?" He looked deeply into her eyes. "If you've come home, why can't you stay?"

"My job ... Roberto's ... Beverly Hills ... my roommates ..." She felt herself getting lost in his eyes as she recited her listless list.

"What about your job here? Hair and Now? Your family? *Me?*"

"You ... ?" She blinked.

"Yes. *Me ... and you.*" He leaned in to kiss her ... and without hesitation she kissed him back.

Now she felt even dizzier than before—and happier than she'd ever been.

"You *are* home, Rita." Johnny pushed a strand of hair away from her face. "Can't you see that?"

She slowly nodded as she thought of her ice-skating dream three weeks ago ... and how it all seemed to be fitting into place. "Yes, I think I'm just beginning to see it."

"Welcome home." He leaned down to kiss her again.

"Happy Valentine's Day," she whispered back.

If you enjoyed *Love Gently Falling*, look for
Melody Carlson's Valentine's Day novel

Once Upon a Winter's Heart

Emma Burcelli concludes that love is officially dead when her grandfather, Poppi, suddenly passes, leaving her grandmother, Nona, devastated. To help out, Emma works in the family bookstore. Although
she feels like a V-Day Scrooge, Emma quickly learns to enjoy the task
of decorating the store for Valentine's Day with the help of a handsome family friend, Lane Forester. As Emma and Lane share time and
memories of Poppi, she reconsiders the notion that romance is *alive*.

Just as Emma's heart begins to lift, however, she learns her sister
has already staked a claim on Lane. Emma's mother and sister insist
that Lane sees her only as a future sister-in-law, but she can't help
wondering if it could be something more.

CENTER
STREET

Available now from Center Street wherever books are sold.

Turn this page for a preview of
Once Upon a Winter's Heart.

Chapter 1

"Romance is officially dead," Emma Burcelli proclaimed as she reached for the last empty crate. She pulled off the lid and dropped several pairs of jeans into the plastic box, packing them down.

"That is so coldhearted." Lucy frowned as she handed Emma a small stack of wool sweaters. "Why would you say that?"

Emma looked sadly at her roommate—her soon-to-be ex-roommate. "Because my grandparents were the last of the true romantics and now my grandfather is gone." She let out a long sigh. "I honestly don't know what my grandmother will do without Poppi. Those two were inseparable. I doubt they ever spent a night apart."

"How old is your grandmother?" Lucy handed her the plastic lid.

"I think she's eighty-six now." Emma snapped the lid into place. "They just celebrated sixty-five years last summer. And they both seemed in such good health...I felt certain they'd make it to their seventieth anniversary." Emma stood. "But now Nona is having some health problems, and today she forgot to take her blood pressure meds. My mom's predicting Nona won't last long on her own. I've heard it's not so unusual, I mean, when a couple has enjoyed such a good marriage, that one partner follows the other within the year."

"I'm sorry about your grandfather." Lucy shook her head.

"And that's why I need to go. Nona was like a second mom to me when I was growing up, when my parents were so busy with their careers. I couldn't forgive myself if she passed on too without me getting to spend some time with her." Emma set the last crate onto the stack by the door. "But I hate leaving you in the lurch like this, Lucy. Are you sure you can find someone to share the apartment?"

"I already told you it's okay, Em. Family is important— you need to go. And there's always someone at work looking for something in the city. If I get a girl in here right away I can reimburse you for February."

Emma hugged Lucy. "Thanks for being so understanding."

"Let me help you get this stuff down to your car." Lucy picked up a crate.

After several trips, the compact Prius was packed to the gills and it was time to go. Emma gave Lucy one last hug, blinking back tears. "I'm gonna miss you, Lucy."

"Me too." Lucy's eyes filled. "You better get out of here if you want to beat the commuter traffic."

"Yeah, and I want to get home before dark." Emma got into her car and, giving the old apartment complex one last glance, she waved to Lucy. Really, she reminded herself as she backed out the car, she was overdue for a change. She'd enjoyed her time in Seattle... at first... but these last couple of years had been nothing but disappointing. And she would not miss her job at all. Selling badly illustrated, poorly written, and overly sentimental e-cards was not the career she'd dreamed of while securing her degree in marketing. It was not what she'd signed on for when she'd joined the so-called up-and-coming Seattle marketing firm. They called themselves BrightPond, but DullPond would better describe that company and the "boys" who ran it.

As Emma drove down the freeway she tried to distract herself from feeling blue about Poppi by listening to the radio. But when an Adele heartbreak song started to play, she turned it off and let out a loud sigh. Okay, she knew it was somewhat cold and hard to go around proclaiming that romance was dead, but that was exactly how she felt inside. Not only because Poppi had died, although that placed a definite exclamation mark on her opinionated statement, but also because of her own personal experiences. Too many times she'd discovered that men like her grandfather were all but nonexistent. Truly Poppi had been the last of a dying breed.

Of course, she knew that Poppi would probably argue this with her. He would launch into a passionate lecture about how love was alive and well for those who were willing to take notice. "Just open your eyes," he would often say to people, "love is all around you." But Emma had never been able to see it. Poppi had been lucky in the romance arena. He'd met Nona, the love of his life, in Napoli shortly after World War II—the war that had devastated much of Italy. But despite losing family and suffering deprivations, they'd managed to hold on to this wonderful sense of optimism and hope and love. Shortly after marrying, they immigrated to America, starting new lives in Seattle near some of Nona's relatives. Later on they moved their little family to a small town in the mountains, and they opened a bookstore in the 1960s.

Her grandparents' story had always sounded so romantic to Emma as she was growing up that for years she believed something that wonderful and magical would happen to her...someday. In fact, she had fully expected it. But after more than a decade of disappointing relationships, most of which she preferred not to remember at all, Emma had grown seriously jaded about love and romance...and men in general. Most of the men she'd dated had proven to be self-absorbed, shallow, and immature. Whether it was just bad luck or bad choices, she'd eventually grown weary of dating in general. And over the years she'd become increasingly certain that good, decent, chivalrous men, like an endangered species, no longer existed in the real world. True romance was only to be found in old movies and classic books.

Even Emma's parents seemed to have missed out in the love and romance department. For as long as Emma could remember they'd bickered and fought over almost everything. The fact they were still together probably had more to do with the image they liked to maintain than real love. With highly visible careers, her parents thrived on keeping up appearances. Although they shared the same building on Main Street, with her dad's law practice on the first floor and her mom's design firm up above, anyone who knew Saundra and Rob Burcelli personally knew that this couple lived very separate lives. And anyone who knew them really well, like their close relatives, knew that Rob and Saundra slept in separate bedrooms. Emma's mom claimed it was due to Rob's snoring, but Emma knew better. And, really, it wasn't all that surprising. For as long as she could recall Emma had known and accepted that her parents' marriage was nothing like Nona and Poppi's.

Tired of these depressing thoughts, Emma turned the radio back on. Even listening to sad love songs was preferable to getting bummed out like this. But now that she was off the freeway and heading into the foothills, the Seattle station was breaking up. Plus it was starting to rain. Turning off the radio, she knew it was time to focus on her driving. At these elevations and this time of year, it could be icy out here.

It was just getting dusky when she pulled up to Nona's house. The familiarity of the Craftsman style home glowing in the rosy twilight welcomed Emma just as it had always done. Despite the frosty air, the bungalow's windows seemed to promise golden warmth and respite and love. How many times had she and her younger sister arrived at this haven in search of refuge? Only now . . . things had changed. Poppi was gone.

She swallowed against the lump in her throat as she parked in front of the house. But as she got out of the car, she was slightly taken aback by the sight of her mother's late model Cadillac in the driveway. What was she doing here at this time of day? As Emma hurried up to the house, she grew worried. Had Nona's health gotten worse? Her mom had mentioned that Nona had neglected to take her blood pressure medicine yesterday. What if she'd suffered a stroke or heart attack today? It was bad enough that Emma hadn't been able to say goodbye to Poppi. But what if Nona was gone as well?

She ran up the porch steps and, knocking on the door, waited a moment before testing to see if it was locked, which would be highly unusual. Then Emma let herself in. "Nona?" she called softly. "Hello? *Mom?*"

"Oh, there you are." Saundra Burcelli rushed toward her, smelling like Obsession perfume and looking typically elegant in her pale blue cashmere sweater set and freshwater pearls. She held her arms open and hugged Emma. "Welcome home, darling. Did you have a good drive?"

"Yes," Emma said quickly. "Is Nona okay?" She peeled off her parka, glancing anxiously around the living room. Everything looked pretty much the same. Except that Poppi's recliner was sadly empty. She turned away, unwilling to break into tears again.

"Nona is fine. I made sure she took her medicine today. And she's resting right now." Her mom tipped her head toward the closed bedroom door on the other end of the living room. "It's been a long day for her. Tending to arrangements for the memorial service and all that. I told her that I could handle it for her, but she insisted on being involved with every last tiny detail. She wants everything to be just perfect for Poppi."

"I got here as quickly as I could." Emma hung her parka on the hall tree by the door. "And I can help her with everything that needs doing from here on out, Mom."

"I'm still surprised they let you off work in the middle of the week like this, Emma. And with such short notice." Saundra peered curiously at her. "I was under the impression you worked for some horrible slave driver."

"As a matter of fact, my boss refused to let me take time off." Emma stuck her chin out defiantly. "And so I quit."

"You *quit*?" Her mother's blue eyes widened in alarm.

"I've hated working there almost from the get-go." Emma lowered her voice and moved away from her grandmother's bedroom door. "I've been considering leaving them for over a year now."

"But in this economy, Emma? Can you really afford to do that?"

Emma shrugged. "I wanted to be free to help Nona. But not just for a week like you suggested. Now I can stay as long as she needs me. I'll help her with household chores and I can drive her to appointments and to the grocery store and whatever—just like Poppi used to do. And I can help with the bookstore too."

"Yes..." Her mom sounded doubtful. "And I'm sure she'll appreciate all that. But don't forget Virginia and Cindy still work at the bookstore."

"I know, but without Poppi around to manage things...well, the bookstore might suffer."

"But I don't like to see you sacrificing your career for—"

"My career was sacrificing itself." Emma ran her finger through some dust on the mantel. "That marketing firm was going absolutely nowhere, Mom. And I was going nowhere with them. I needed a break...a chance to regroup and refocus. You know?"

Saundra made an uncertain nod. "If you say so."

"What's that smell?" Emma sniffed the air. "Is something burning?"

"Oh, fiddlesticks!" Her mom turned to the kitchen. "I was attempting to make us some dinner and I completely forgot to—"

"You're cooking?" Emma tried not to sound too alarmed as she followed her mom through the dining room and into the kitchen.

Saundra bent to open the oven door, using a dishtowel to wave away the smoke now billowing out. Meanwhile Emma turned on the exhaust fan over the stove and peered down at what looked like a blackened animal of some kind. "What is it?" she asked.

"It was going to be roasted chicken. But I forgot to turn the timer on to remind me to turn the temperature down. It was only supposed to be that high for five minutes." She scowled at the clock. "It's been at least forty-five."

"Oh..." Emma grimaced. "Is there any saving it? Maybe we could peel off the burnt layer and—"

"No." Her mom shoved the forlorn bird back into the oven and, firmly closing the door, she turned off the oven. "Fortunately we have lots of casseroles and other dishes in the fridge. Everyone has been very generous with your grandmother. I just thought it would be nice to have a roasted chicken, *that's all*."

"Maybe I should take over from here," Emma suggested. "I mean if you need to go home and fix Dad's dinner. Or do you ever do that anymore...I mean cook at home?" Emma's mother had never been into cooking, but even so she usually ate dinner with Rob.

"I know what you're thinking, Emma Jane. But it may interest you to know that my cooking skills have improved of late. I even took a French cuisine class at the community college last fall." Her mom patted her platinum blonde hair into place as if she were getting ready to pose for the cover of a new cookbook.

"*French* cuisine?" Emma frowned as she reached for a dishcloth. "What's wrong with learning to cook Italian food?" Emma had grown up hearing her father bemoaning the fact that his wife refused to learn how to make the simplest Italian dishes. Saundra Burcelli couldn't even make decent spaghetti. Of course, her mom's usual reaction to her dad's complaints was to angrily tell him if he wanted Italian food, he could go to his parents' house to eat. And sometimes he did, because everyone knew that Nona always had something delicious bubbling away in her little old-fashioned kitchen.

Her mom scowled. "What's wrong with French cuisine?"

"Nothing." Emma glanced around the messy kitchen. Hopefully Nona hadn't seen it like this. Was all this chaos the result of her mother's attempt to simply roast a chicken? "But, really, Mom, if you need to go home and take care of—"

"I do not *need* to go home," her mom said sharply.

"Okay..." Emma started clearing the counters and straightening the kitchen, all the while wondering why her mother was in such a foul mood right now. Certainly, she was sad over Poppi's sudden demise... but then so was everyone.

"As a matter of fact, I do not plan to go home at all," her mother abruptly declared.

Emma paused from wiping the countertop. *"Wh-what?"*

Saundra turned away from Emma. Fussing with the old spice rack, she meticulously turned each little jar to face out. "I wasn't certain you were coming, Emma," she said slowly. "So I have, uh... well, I've made plans to stay with Nona for a while myself."

"But I *told* you I was coming—and that I'd be here this evening." Emma dropped the dishrag into the sink and placed a hand on her mother's shoulder, forcing her to turn around, face to face. Locking eyes with Saundra, Emma was determined to get to the bottom of this. "You *knew* that, Mom. So why are you acting like you didn't? Or that you need to be here when you knew I was on my way? What's up?"

Her mother looked uneasy as she fingered her pearls, pressing her lips tightly together as if trying to come up with an appropriate answer.

"What is going on, Mom?" Emma studied Saundra closely... something was not right.

"Nothing's going on." Saundra looked down.

"I can tell something's wrong. What is it?"

Saundra folded her arms across her front with a stubborn look.

"Does this have to do with Dad?" Emma demanded. "Did you guys get in a fight?"

"Fine. If you must know, *I've left your father.*"

"*What?*" Emma blinked. In all the years...all the fights...her mom had never left her dad before. Not that Emma knew of anyway.

"You heard what I said, Emma. I've left him. I'm finished. I'm done." Her mother's lower lip trembled slightly as she reached for a tissue from the box that Nona always kept on top of the old refrigerator.

"But why?"

"*Why?*" She looked at Emma with teary eyes. "Because—because it's over—that's why. And please, do not tell Nona about this. She is already stressed over losing Poppi and there's her blood pressure to consider. I don't want her to find out that her only son is a miserable excuse of a husband—not to mention a cad." And now she turned away and hurried from the room.

Emma just stood there feeling dazed. Poppi had died yesterday. And now her parents' marriage was over as well? Not to mention Nona's health was suffering. What more bad news awaited her? She hadn't heard from her younger sister yet...hopefully Anne and her son, Tristan, were okay— although the recent divorce had probably taken its toll on both of them. Emma shook her head sadly as she opened the old fridge. Perusing the assortment of covered Tupperware containers and casserole dishes, trying to find something suitable for dinner, Emma realized that her family was quickly coming unraveled.

Praise for Melody Carlson

Once Upon a Winter's Heart

"A sweet, quick read that celebrates love's beginnings as well the spirit of Valentine's Day."

—Serena Chase, USAToday.com

"A delightful story about the loss and recovery of romance, love and hope...*Once Upon a Winter's Heart* will revive anyone who's given up on romance and wants a happy ending."

—*Family Fiction*

"Melody delivers all that is sweetest and best about love in this Valentine's novella and does it with a tasty dash of Italian spice. Now that's amore!"

—Robin Jones Gunn, bestselling author of *Sisterchicks in Gondolas*

"A sweet love story, *Once Upon a Winter's Heart* is a beautiful picture of the joy of being swept off your feet."

—Melanie Dobson, award-winning author of *Love Finds You in Mackinac Island, Michigan*, and *Where the Trail Ends*

The Christmas Pony

"Delightful...Should be on everyone's must-read list for the holiday season."

—*RT Book Reviews* Top Pick

"A wonderfully sweet story, with vivid descriptions that pull you right into the pages."

—Bookreporter.com

The Christmas Shoppe

"This magical Christmas story is filled with anticipation, holiday traditions and delight...a true gift for the readers."

—*RT Book Reviews*

"A sweet, quick read that celebrates love's beginnings as well the spirit of Valentine's Day."
—Serena Chase, USAToday.com on *Once Upon a Winter's Heart*

Love Gently Falling

Rita Jansen is living her dream as a hairstylist in Hollywood when her father calls with news that her mother has suffered a stroke. When she gets home to Chicago, Rita finds her mother is healing but facing a long recovery. Worse, without being able to run their family-owned salon, her mother could lose the business. Rita decides to help, but she only has until Valentine's Day to come up with a plan.

As Rita takes her mother's place at work, the nearby skating rink she loved as a child brings back fond memories. Rita also finds herself renewing friendships with her childhood best friend, Marley, as well as her classmate Johnny. Although they now lead such seemingly different lives, Rita is surprised by how well she and Johnny connect and how far he will go to help her. Though Rita believes Johnny is only being kind, with romance kindling in the air and on the ice, their friendship may just fall into something more.

HEEYSUN RUETTGERS

MELODY CARLSON is a bestselling and award-winning author of more than 200 books for adults and young readers. She and her husband live in the beautiful Pacific Northwest with their dog, Audrey. Visit her website at www.melodycarlson.com.

BOOKish For more about this book and author, visit Bookish.com

FICTION
www.centerstreet.com
Also available as an ebook
Cover illustration by Mark Stutzman
Cover design by JuLee Brand
Cover © 2015 Hachette Book Group, Inc.
Printed in the U.S.A.

$12.00 US / $13.00 CAN.
ISBN 978-1-4555-2810-3

51200

9 781455 528103